# FIRST TIME GAY

## AN 8 BOOK COLLECTION

### DICK WILDER

# CHAPTER 1
# BREAK ME OPEN

Joseph

THAT MAN IS SO FUCKING sexy. That man, is the only man that I want to be inside of my dark, hot asshole.

That man is not someone who I *should* want - but he is someone that I do want. I'd give anything to be with him - I'd sacrifice anything to be alone with him, to be naked with him, to be able to taste him and to be able to feel him deep inside of my ass. I want to tease him, to push my cock into his face and let him lick and suck my hardness, and I want to climb on top of him, letting him slide inside of me - riding him and then holding onto him - keeping him inside of my asshole and making him cum.

I want him to make me his. I want to hear him say that he likes guys more than he likes girls.

. . .

I want him to leave his wife for me, I want us to get married and adopt kids, so that we can raise our children together. Then, we'll hire someone to babysit for us, so that we can go out on dates.

Just like he and his wife hire me, to babysit for them.

I know, I KNOW! I really shouldn't be fantasizing about him - there's no way that a 40 year old man would be interested in me, a 21 year old guy - right? I mean I'm cute and everything, I've got long toned legs, I've got a muscled chest, and I'm always being told that I'm attractive... but why would he want to fuck me? I'm sure that he just likes his wife, or at least women his age.

I'm being a silly boy, I know it. My fantasies should just stay as fantasies...

Dave

Hot fucking damn I want to fuck the shit out of that boy.

I don't know what's wrong with me. Is this my mid-life crisis? I don't think it is, I'd want to fuck him no matter how old I was. I've always been attracted to guys but he just makes me wild. If I were 21 like him, I'd be more open about my sexualirt - I'd ask him on a date, or I'd spend an age trying to be friends with him, just to get a hug from him, just to feel his cock getting hard through his clothes against me, then I'd go and masturbate thinking about him.

Now? Now I just want to rip into him. Tear off his clothes, and suck on his youthful balls and his bulging dick. I just want to feed my cock into his mouth and hold his head against me, making him gag on me - before spinning him around, bending him over and fucking his tight asshole hard.

Jesus, I may as well be a teenager. I'm not even his friend, I just drive him home after he's babysat for us. I'm pathetic, when he's sitting next to me I 'accidentally' brush his leg with my hand, pretending to be reaching for the gear stick. I position myself so that I'm sitting closer to him than I typically would be to my own wife. I inhale deeply when he's in the car, smelling his sweet, young scent. I stare at his ass when he's getting out of the car, and then I rush home, jump in the shower and spank my meat while thinking about him.

The other day, when he was getting out of the car and when I was staring at his ass - as usual - I saw the top line of his briefs, riding up over the tops of his jeans. They were a sexy deep blue color, they turned me on so much, and I found myself alone in the car with a raging boner.

I just couldn't wait. I'd smelled him, I'd brushed his leg, and I'd seen the color of his underpants. I couldn't hold it until I got home, I had to masturbate in the car.

. . .

It was risky, but I didn't give a fuck. I reached over to the glove box and pulled out a fast food napkin, then unzipped myself and pulled out my cock. I was still driving, and had just turned onto the highway when I wrapped that napkin around my hard dick and stroked myself, the image of his deep blue underpants burned into my mind, his masculine yet sweet sexy scent still in my nostrils.

I must have been swerving all over the place, leaning back in my seat - tugging on my cock, thinking about Joseph. 'God I want you' I whispered into the car, 'I want your ass, I want my cock deep inside of your sweet little asshole!' I drove and stroked, my eyes basically closing as I imagined him on top of me, his young chest in my face, his arms wrapped around me - his lips next to my ear, begging for me to cum inside of him. I slowed the car way down as I came close, breathlessly tugging on my cock, fucking *feeling* him with me as I shot my load into that napkin.

Man, I'd obviously tossed myself off thinking about him, but this was something that felt different. He had been in my car just a few minutes before, and now I had shot my load in there, thinking about him. Ridiculous I know, but it almost felt as though we had actually fucked, that I had actually shot my cum deep into his tight young asshole.

I wonder what his asshole actually feels like. Is he tight? Is he warm? Does he grip onto cock while a guy is fucking him?

And what is his cock really like? I've seen him in shorts before, and he seems to have quite a package but is he thick?

Is he cut or uncut? And what about his balls... are they smooth or hairy? Are they big enough to wrap my lips around and suck?

Fuck - I really, REALLY need to do something about this. I'm not interested in my wife at all, not that she cares, but even if she offered herself to me I don't even know if I would get hard. She could be lying naked on the bed and begging me to fuck her, and I bet that my cock would only be semi-erect. Seeing a small sample of Joseph's underpants, and I'm at full mast.

Maybe Joseph would want me... maybe he's been waiting for me to make the first move? But it's such a risk, I could lose everything...

Just one sign. One sign from him and I'll jump. I'll fuck him hard and I'll empty my load deep inside of him. Just one sign...

Joseph

I can't take it any longer.

The other day, he drove me home after I babysat, as he usually does. I always make sure to sit close to the center console, and he usually touches my leg when he puts his hand on that shifter stick thing.

· · ·

I fucking love it when he does that. It makes me feel like he does it on purpose, like he actually wants me. I know it's probably just me being silly, but it feels like he reaches over to me, and that he leaves his hand there a little longer than he should if it were really an accident.

That night it seemed like there was some energy in the car. It honestly felt as though we both wanted the same thing - and what I wanted was for him to pull that car over, lean closer to me and to kiss me. I could feel my breaths getting heavier, my chest heaving, blood pumping to my cock as he drove down the highway.

That wasn't what really got me excited, though. When we got to my house, and he paid me for the babysitting, he seemed to lean into me. His eyes were all over my body, and when I opened the door and got out, I realized that my jeans had come down a little and that the top of my underpants were on show to him.

I looked behind me as I closed the door, seeing that his eyes were firmly fixed on my ass. He had a look of pure desire on his face, his mouth was slightly open - his tongue licking his bottom lip.

God fucking damn, I should have acted right there and then. I should have got back in the car and told him to drive some-where secluded, so that I could suck his cock in the back of the car and then bent over the seat to let him fuck me from behind. I rushed quickly into my house, not even bothering to say anything to my parents but running upstairs to my room.

. . .

I tugged my shirt over my head, my hands rubbing against my smooth chest and my little sensitive nipples as I imagined him standing behind me, his hands where mine were - his tongue lapping at my neck, sending shivers and goosebumps across my body. I unbuttoned my jeans and pulled them down, my cock already hard - my fingers sliding down my thin body - rushing quickly towards my groin.

I stood, still feeling that he was close to me, practically feeling his cock pressing into my back as the fingers of one hand stroked my dick and reached further, to slid up and down the sensitive opening of my asshole - teasing me, before starting to stroke stronger - allowing my thumb to slide softly into the warm pocket of my ass. I gasped as I entered into myself, my eyes rolling back in my head as I rubbed, finger fucking myself - while thinking about him. That look he'd given to my ass had sent me over the edge and now that I was imagining myself with him, I was sending myself over the edge. My hand was gripping my cock strongly, stroking it - sending me to the very edge of an orgasm that was being controlled by a man who was miles away from me, probably now on the highway - heading back to his house and to his wife.

Fuck her. Fuck that bitch, he's mine now. I opened my legs wider, grasping at my flesh - stroking myself frantically, dipping my fingers into my asshole as a massive orgasm consumed me. God fucking damn that felt good, my body tingling, my desires flowing wildly as I came with a muffled shout, begging for that man to cum inside of my tight, hot ass.

. . .

One sign. Just one sign from him, and I'll jump. I'll strip for him, I'll let him touch me, I'll beg him to let me suck him, and I'll open up my dank asshole for him - and make sure that he cums deep inside of me.


Dave


Fuck it. I can't go on like this for much longer - I'm going to go wild. The wife is away at a conference, it's time to test the waters…. To see if he's at all open to the idea of a fuck.


I decided to text him - one evening when the kids were already asleep, but pretending that I had work to do and needed someone who could put them back to bed if they happened to wake up.


'Only if that's okay' I said in a message to him, once he'd said that he would be happy to come over. 'I - you know - don't want to spoil your night, in case you have a date or something'.


'Oh no' he responded - 'No date, I'm totally single.'


That imaginary sound effect that played in my head was a door opening….

•  •  •

'You're kidding me!' I texted back. 'I'm surprised, a cute guy like yourself'.

'Well' he said, 'I don't really go for guys my age… I prefer older men'.

Holy fuck, this is going too well!

'Any guy would be lucky to be with you' I said, pacing around the house as I typed, deleting messages before sending them, then writing them out again. Pretty soon I was going to say something that was out there - that really told him that I wanted to fuck his tight asshole. 'You're pretty awesome, you know that right?'

'Awe' he replied - 'Thank you, that means so much. Especially coming from you…'

Oh jesus… I can feel my cock getting hard here. I keep pushing the envelope, he keeps on coming back with more and more sexy words.

'Me? Hell Joseph, I'm sure you'd want way more than me…'

We're getting close… there's only so much that can be said now.

. . .

'Oh, I wouldn't say that ;)'


A fucking winky face! Man, I haven't felt my cock get this hard in so long! It was time to go for it, to really tell him what I thought. Here goes nothing, it's now or never!


'I'd give anything to be with you, you should know that…'


Fuck. Radio silence. The previous messages had been responded too quickly, but this one? Nothing coming back. i'd gone too far, I'd said something that I really shouldn't have said. What now? Would he tell my wife? Would he tell his parents? His dad is a mean looking bastard, he'd probably give me a fucking black eye and I wouldn't blame him! Oh fuck, I've really done it now, I'm totally fucked and who is at the door at this hour?


I went downstairs, trying not to look as panicked as I felt. I'd deal with whoever was at my front door, and then I'd figure out what to do.


I opened the door, to see a very familiar face. Joseph was standing there, a taxi pulling out of the driveway. He was grinning from ear to ear, and he jumped towards me as soon as I opened the door.


'Anything huh?' he said, whispering into my ear as he wrapped his arms around me. I held him on the doorstep, burying my face into his hair, smelling him - taking in his warmth and holding him close to me, his groin grazing against mine - letting me feel his growing cock as he embraced me. 'I don't want much... I do want you to cum inside me though...'

I pulled him into the house, our hands both all over each other - mine rushing to his ass and clutching him as our lips met. Tongues intertwined, his minty breath tasted so fresh as we made out like teenagers. I kneaded his ass cheeks as he went for my belt buckle, flipping it open quickly and tugging at my jeans until they fell south. Damn I was so fucking hard for him, and it was all *for* him - my cock had belonged to his mouth and his ass for longer than he knew.

I slid my fingers into the back of his jeans, twisting them around the band of his underpants. I didn't know if it was the same pair that I'd seen, but they seemed at least to be the same design - my hands excited to tug at the elastic - knowing that they would be putting a gentle level of pressure on his cock, his balls, and his asshole.

God, making out with him was fucking amazing - he delved deep into my mouth with his tongue then gently bit my bottom lip, his hands busy with the band of my briefs. My cock was fucking pulsating inside of my underwear, and as he pulled them down with a flourish I felt my dick springing towards him. He reached for it with his hand, wrapping his fingers around my meaty girth and stroking me, before breaking his mouth away from mine, smiling at me - winking - and then slowly dropping to his knees.

. . .

My head flew back as my hands followed him down - we were still in the hallway of my house as he held my cock upright, his hot breath hitting my balls as his tongue extended to lick the tip of my cock. Just feeling his mouth on my dick made me groan as he rolled my head with his tongue before sliding it up and down my length - rustling in my balls before sliding back to the tip - opening his mouth - and letting me inside.

Fucking damn he was so good at this - his tongue lapping around my thick cock while his lips closed around it - sucking on me strongly, that tongue performing fucking miracles as he went to town. My hands quickly came to the back of his head - holding him in place as my hips gyrated, letting my dick steam into him - skull fucking him as he opened his mouth wide to let my cock feel the back of his throat.

'Fucking DAMN Joseph! I could fucking cum now! Jesus your mouth is so good, I could cum down your throat!'

Joseph

I kinda knew that he was liking it…

My tongue was so busy with his cock - teasing him and then taking him fully in. He tasted so good, and I wanted to taste his cum too…

. . .

But a deal is a deal, right? And I wasn't going to let him cum anywhere until I'd felt him explode deep inside of my dank asshole. My body wouldn't forgive me if I let anything else happen!

I could feel him growing in my mouth - beginning to pulsate, his balls tightening as he came close to orgasm. I gently released him from the grip that my lips were creating - then stood and turned, walking slowly towards the living room and to the back of the leather couch where I would often lie, fantasizing about being with him. Slowly, knowing that he was behind me and was watching me, I took down my pants and peeled my tight underpants over my ass cheeks - then leaned over the back of the couch with my legs open - offering my bare, glistening ass to him. As one last act of encouragement I turned my head to him, saying 'Come - now. Fuck me, take me, use my hot asshole. My ass is all yours... all you've got to do is cum inside of me, okay?' - and I then put my head down into the couch, burying it in the cushions.

I had figured that he would reach me quickly - I didn't plan on him practically bounding towards me! His hand smacked onto my ass cheeks quickly - stinging my flesh as his fingers gripped onto my ass, parting me - his thumb roughly digging at my hole to prepare it for his cock.

His other hand came to my waist, bracing me - before that thick cock pushed at my opening. Damn I was so fucking horny - my asshole opened immediately for him - almost sucking his cock inside as he pushed, easing that thick dick deep into my willing hole.

·  ·  ·

'Fucking hell Joseph - you're so fucking tight! And so fucking hot! I'm gonna cum so quickly in you - I'm gonna cum deep inside of you!'

God damn, he threw that hard cock into me so fast that my cock scraped on the cushions of the couch, my sensitive balls sending shouts of joy to my brain as my ass got so stretched out, feeling him filling me entirely. He steamed into me, slamming his weight deep inside, stretching my ass as his hands rained down onto my body. His palms slapping my ass cheeks as he fucked me so hard, so strong, so fast - I groaned with pleasure as he used me - using my tight asshole to make his cock cum.

'Harder!' I gasped, sweat running across my face, my whole body shaking as I felt my orgasm consuming every fiber of my body. 'Fuck me! Cum in me! Fuck me hard!'

He pummeled that thick girth into me, I could feel every inch of him as he entered and withdrew, slapped and grabbed onto every available piece of flesh that he could reach. I felt a single drop of his sweat as it fell from his brow to the small of my back, then his cock exploding inside of me, delivering his hot cum - filling my asshole to the brim with his seed - just as my own dick spurted, sending my cum onto the leather seats below me.

Holy fucking damn, was that a night to remember... and pretty soon, we'd be doing something *even more* amazing!

# CHAPTER 2
# TWINK SITTER

'AWW' I said, walking to the bookshelf. 'This bear is so cute!'

I was suddenly feeling so comfortable and so confident. Rare for me, I have always been such a shy guy but as soon as I hit 20 years of age I started to realize that I needed to come out of my shell a little bit.

'It is, isn't it?' Mr. Thomas said, walking with me and picking up the bear. The bear was about 12 inches in height and as he turned the bear to face me I noticed that it had eyes that seemed to actually look at me. 'It's actually pretty clever'.

I liked Mr. Thomas as soon as I met him. Have you ever done that? You meet someone and immediately feel a kind of connection with them? He put me at ease as soon as he responded to my first text and I very quickly knew that he was going to be a good person in my life.

I had answered an online ad that he had placed for a babysitter. Just a few months ago I wouldn't have bothered to respond to it, I would have thought to myself 'no one will want to have a young gay guy looking after their kids' - but now - now I'm more likely to take a chance to get something that I want. And I have always loved to watch kids, I used to babysit a little bit when I was younger, but hadn't for a couple of years. Now I have a job at a clothing store in the mall but I have found that I have a lot of spare time - especially in the evenings.

I don't have a boyfriend. I've actually never had a boyfriend and I've never had sex. That's not entirely by choice, I like guys, I've known that I'm gay since forever ago and I like to play with myself and bring myself to orgasm - and I have always wanted to know what it feels like to actually fuck - but I have just never been in a position to do it.

I'm cute, I guess. I'm short, 5'6" and that has always affected my confidence but I have an attractive face and a pretty good body. I work out, and if I'm honest I always wanted to make myself attractive to other guys but I never actually wanted to fuck them - but I didn't want to be naked in front of them because…

Well, I have to be truthful here… I didn't want to be naked in front of them because my cock was so small.

I know, it happens, some people just develop later than others but I honestly thought that I was always going to be small. I would always make sure that I was entirely covered up in changing rooms, not wanting anyone to see how small my dick was but thankfully, wonderfully, about a year ago it began to grow.

It's not huge, but from what I've seen from porn videos and stuff I'm a little bigger than average and that's good enough for me. My cock looks good, especially when it's hard, and I have balls that I love to play with. They are so sensitive! I swear to you right now, if I ever do get a boyfriend then the first thing I'll ask him to do is to suck on my balls because I'm pretty sure that if they were sucked on, I'd cum immediately. Now that I'm more comfortable with my body I'm on a charge to find a man who will lie naked with me and suck my balls, and my cock.

It really was a lack of confidence that stopped me from getting out there and meeting people or even getting a boyfriend. I know that I'm cute and I see guys looking at me, especially at the gya friendly gym that I go to, but I didn't have the nerve to approach anyone and on the few occasions that anyone came to talk to me and flirt with me, I turned into such a gibbering wreck that they must have thought I was entirely stupid and embarrassing to be seen with.

So I turned 20, and I told myself rather sternly that I had to change myself. I got a job in a clothing store which meant that I had to deal with members of the public and that really helped, and I started to volunteer for a local animal shelter. My outlook changed, in fact my expression changed - where I previously often looked like I was always in a fowl fucking mood I was now more sunny, more attractive, more approachable. I began to feel that it was only a matter of time - that someone awesome would soon walk into my life.

I just didn't think that the awesome person would be a guy who was married with kids.

I saw his ad for a babysitter and texted that evening, seeing that they lived pretty close to me. He did actually mentioned in his ad that he was one side of a gay relationship - two guys with their two kids who wanted someone gay friendly to watch their kids. Well I thought to myself that there's no-one more gay friendly than a gay guy, and extra money isn't anything to turn down, and I had always enjoyed babysitting so overall it was a no brainer for me. Getting such nice responses from him was just the icing on the cake.

And then I met him. And my knees went weak.

He opened the door to me with a generous smile and an outstretched arm which beckoned me into his house. He was dressed so nicely and as I walked past him and into the hallway I could smell his cologne which was so musky and sexy and made me want to ask him right there and then if I could suck his cock.

Of course I didn't - but dirty thoughts ran through my mind as he showed me into the house, into the living room with its beautiful brown leather couch, and into the kitchen.

The conversation flowed as he told me about their kids and what they wanted me to do. Basically 'not much' overall, they wanted me to be there when they went out on a Thursday night for a date - they would put their kids to bed before I got there, so they just expected me to watch their TV and eat their snacks until they got home. Easy, and if it meant that I would see the sexy Mr. Thomas every week then that all sounded to me like it would be a great deal.

'Let me just show you their room' he said, smiling that sexy smile at me and leading me towards the stairs. 'Just so that you know where they are'.

That's where I saw the bear on the bookshelf that he was now holding in his hands.

'It looks like it's looking right at me!' I said in wonderment as I held the bear in my hands. I moved from side to side and saw that his eyes really did seem to move when I did.

'Well, he kind of is' Mr. Thomas said with a smile as he took his cell phone from his pocket. He opened an app and showed me his phone screen. On the screen I saw my face, and I realized that the eyes of the bear were actually video cameras, which were sending video to his phone. 'It's a nanny cam, I guess that's what they call it. It just means that I can keep an eye on the kids. So when I'm downstairs, if I want to make sure that they are asleep I can just check on my phone instead of coming up here'.

'That's awesome' I said, handing it back to him. 'So useful'.

As he took the bear from me our fingers touched. What should have been a totally innocent touch turned my legs to jelly as I looked at him, seeing that he was looking down at my body with a seductive gaze and then into my eyes. I felt my heart beat faster and harder, my skin suddenly breaking out in goosebumps as I moved slightly closer to him, very slowly but very deliberately - ready to give him whatever he wanted.

'BILL!' came a shrill voice from downstairs. 'BILL WHERE THE FUCK ARE YOU?'

His gaze flickered away from mine and rolled to the back of his head. Clearly annoyed, he sighed loudly and put the bear back onto the bookshelf.

'The other half' he said, with a shrug. 'Andrew. He's downstairs, by the sounds of things. He'll want to meet you, though you might not want to meet him'.

Uh oh. Was there trouble in paradise? Was this a little bit of a green light to me to get up to some mischief with Mr. Thomas? As much as I had lusted after him just a few minutes earlier I honestly didn't think that I could really mess around with someone who was happily married. But - if his husband was actually the asshole that he sounded like he was - maybe I wouldn't be so much in the wrong?

I didn't like Andrew at all, those first impressions certainly weren't anything like those that I had about his husband. He stood downstairs and barely acknowledged me, but scowled at his husband instead.

I did think that he looked pretty attractive, sexy even. Not nearly as hot as his husband but not someone that I would necessarily kick out of my bed - but his attitude turned me off a little. As I left their house and made plans to be back there that Thursday evening, I left with the thought that I would still really really like to lie naked with Bill Thomas, and Andrew could fuck off.

For the days that lead up to my appointment at their house I couldn't get Bill Thomas out of my mind. On the morning of the Thursday he texted me to make sure that I was still okay to babysit for them, and that kicked off a pretty long text conversation. We talked about his job, we talked about my job, and then he asked me a question which got me very interested indeed.

'So… do you have a boyfriend?' he asked, sending that text along with a winky face gif.

'No…' I responded. 'Do you have a boyfriend?'

'Ha! Not a boyfriend no' he texted back. 'It's - you know - complicated'.

'Sometimes things don't have to be complicated…' I said, certainly starting to think that this was now becoming a little bit flirtatious. But… he was married, of course. I couldn't…

'True' he said. 'I do sometimes have some… fun'.

'Interesting' I texted. 'I might like to have some fun someday…'

I swear that I was getting hard just composing and sending these texts. The responses made me blush and made me even more excited. I still didn't know if I could have sex with a married man but his husband was such a shit...

'Remember the bear' he texted back. 'Maybe you could show the bear what you've got underneath your clothes…'

Oh holy shit this was a VERY dirty thought… but I *did* want him, and it was a very sexy idea indeed!

I showered and dressed, making sure that I was wearing my sexiest tight white briefs underneath clothes that were pretty conservative. I didn't want his husband to see me and think that I was trying to get his husband into bed which of course, was absolutely in my plans. I put on my underwear, and then put on jeans and a t-shirt over those scandalous clothes.

When I arrived at their house Bill Thomas greeted me at the door with a smile, and after checking that the coast was clear - a wink. I winked back at him and flashed a sexy smile, until we were both snapped back to some kind of reality by his husband.

'Is he here? Well then let's fucking go, shall we?'

Bill Thomas cleared his throat as his husband put on his shoes.

'I'll - you know - check in with you in about an hour. Sound good?'

'Sounds good' I said in a low voice. 'I'll probably go check on the kids around then, okay?'

We both knew what the plan was and as they pulled away from their house all that I could think about was the sexy Bill Thomas. Obviously we weren't going to fuck that night, how could that ever happen? But I did plan to give him a show and let him know exactly what I had to offer him. I paced around the house before deciding that I should go upstairs and move that bear to a different room, if I was going to strip for Mr. Thomas I probably shouldn't do it in the same room as his kids were sleeping in. I picked it up carefully and carried it into another bedroom which looked like it was a spare room - and placed it gently on a table next to the bed.

I was still so nervous that I stayed in that room, staring at that bear and at my phone. I was waiting for his command, waiting until I knew that he was watching me. It was pretty dark in that room but I didn't want to turn on many lights, in case the neighbors saw and were suspicious that someone was messing around in their house, and I figured that this bear could see in the dark because it was used to keep an eye on the kids at night. A pair of car headlights appeared to slowly pass the house and that gave me enough light to see that the eyes of the bear were suddenly moving.

I looked down at my phone to see that I had a new text.

'I'm watching' it said. 'You look amazing'.

This was my time to shine. He thought I looked good now, just in my jeans cland a t-shirt? Ha! He didn't have any idea what was about to happen. I had thought about this, I knew how I wanted to do this - and I put my sexy little plan into action. I held my phone and selected my media player, putting on a song which flooded out of the speakers.

I wasn't just going to show him my tight white briefs… I was going to dance for him. I was going to strip for him. My plan was to make him so hard and so interested that he would find some excuse to leave his ass of a husband somewhere and come home to fuck me.

I love the song that I played, and as I stood I closed my eyes, my hips swayed from side to side - my hands toying with the base of my shirt. I could feel my excitement rising - knowing that the sexy Bill Thomas was watching me - knowing that he was soon going to see what I was wearing underneath my outer clothing. I turned - my back facing the bear - and unzipped my jeans. I looked over my shoulder - looking at the bear directly in the eyes - winked, and bent over, pulling my jeans down over my ass, revealing my tight briefs and my cute ass.

My phone chirped, as I rose I picked it up and quickly read the message.

'Damn' it said, simply. 'Fucking hell'.

I was so turned on, so in the groove that I didn't respond to the text but smiled at the camera and - biting my bottom lip - whipped off my shirt to reveal my smooth muscled chest. My phone chirped again - the message reading 'Turning on the speaker'. I didn't exactly know what that meant but I continued to dance slowly to the music, knowing that my cock was getting hard, knowing that he would be able to see the outline of my shaft but I was so lost in the music and so full of thoughts of him at that moment that I didn't care, I wanted him so much and I could feel my asshole getting excited as I danced to the music. I suddenly heard a click coming from the bear and sounds coming from it, soft sounds. Moans. male moans.

'Oh yes Bill, yes - yes that's it Bill, lick it, suck it…'

What the fuck was happening here? That sounded like Andrew! It couldn't be... could it?

'We're in the living room' a more familiar voice said - the voice of my crush - Mr. Bill Thomas. 'Come down here Simon - join us'.

The moans from his husband got louder as I began to piece things together. Those headlights that I had seen? They were from Bill and Andrew coming home. This strip show that I had been putting on for him? It had been seen by them both. And now they were downstairs, having sex...

And they wanted me to join them.

Well I did want to fuck Bill. And I did think that his husband was an asshole, but also quite sexy. And I was so horny already...

In all honestly I didn't stop to think for a second. I rushed from that upstairs room and went downstairs, following the sounds of those sexy moans until I reached the living room when I saw them both. Bill Thomas was entirely naked, lying face down - his head buried in his husbands groin. He was also naked except for a pair of socks, his beautiful cock looking so amazing, his erect shaft a beacon to my dirty mind as I crossed the floor, being watched by Andrew who let the phone in his hand drop to the floor.

I knelt beside the couch - letting my hand run along his body and watching as Mr. Thomas used his tongue on his husband - licking the length of his cock, Andrew's thighs closing on Bill's head as his back arched, sending an invitation to me. Bill looked into my eyes, his mouth circling around the tip of Andrew's cock - his hand wrapped around his shaft as he beckoned me to come and join him.

I didn't hesitate to accept that invitation, leaning towards that cock, my tongue coming to join Bill's, both of us kissing at the tip of Andrew's cock and then sliding down his length. I opened my mouth wide to take him in, deep throating as

Bill lapped at my neck, sending shivers throughout my body as I sucked strongly, Bill coming to Andrew's balls, taking one in his mouth with a 'pop' sound, sucking on him as I gagged on the hard cock of his husband. Bill let one hand come to my ass where he grabbed at my briefs, pulling them down over my ass cheeks, his fingers rushing for my puckering, excited asshole - an interested groan coming from his mouth as he prodded at me.

'Damn' he groaned, as he came up for air - circling his tongue around Andrew's quivering belly button, one hand coming up his body to grasp onto the section of his shaft that wasn't in my mouth. 'His ass is as hot as yours and so fucking tight...'

'Do you want to fuck him?' Andrew asked his husband. 'Do you want to fuck him while I watch?'

'I want to' he said, coming back to his cock as my tongue traveled down to Andew's balls - flicking his erect muscle with his tongue while continuing to finger my tight hot asshole. I couldn't quite believe what was happening here... me, a virgin, was sucking on this man's full balls while he was asking his husband if he wanted to fuck me. With each word that came from either of them I just got more and more turned on, my skin bristling, my ass feeling so fucking *empty* as they worked out their agreement.

'Do it' Andrew said - moaning stronger, his hand on the back of my head releasing its grip. 'Simon, do you want to suck me while he fucks you?'

'Oh god yes' I whispered, still with his balls in my mouth as felt Bill coming off the couch and taking a position behind me. As he took the flesh of my briefs in his fingers and stretched them completely over my ass cheek I let my head dive back onto the hard cock of Andrew, letting him fill my mouth - his cock flying deep into my willing throat. Bill Thomas placed his hands on my waist and positioned the tip of his hard cock against my entrance, sliding up and down my ass - playing with me until I had to beg him.

'Please' I uttered, my tongue flicking at Andrew's hardness, widening my stance, slowly and subtly shaking my ass at him - 'please Mr. Thomas, be my first… fuck me, I need to feel your cock inside of me…'

Both of them seemed to be supercharged as I told them that I was a virgin, Andrew picking my head from his cock and holding it in his hands, looking deep into my eyes and smiling at me.

'Fuck him' he ordered. 'Fuck this poor boy, he's a virgin! Take it Bill… take his virginity and fuck him good!'

Bill's grip on my waist tightened as his cock came to me, the tip sliding around my entrance as his husband closed his eyes and opened his mouth, pulling me towards him and locking lips with me as his husband steamed into me. I felt a gasp of amazement as he finally and fully came inside of me, just as his husband's tongue rushed into my mouth. My fingers wrapped around his cock as I stroked him hard, bringing him to the edge of his orgasm as Bill Thomas fucked me deep - fucking hard as I yelped *fucking yelped!* As his fat cock stretched me, pleasured me and took me to the edge of a fast orgasm - his husband's hand leaving my head and coming to my balls where he rolled my so sensitive testicles with his fingers. Bill Thomas sounded like he was getting so close as I rolled my fingers to Andrew's asshole and stuffed two of my fingers inside of him - frantically finger fucking him to orgasm as Bill plunged deep, letting me feel every inch as he pummelled into me - his hands grasping at my flesh as he and his husband made me cum. I whimpered as I came, my body shaking, my face falling onto Andrew's chest as Bill Thomas exited - standing on the couch over us - stroking his cock three times until he gave up his cum - that hot seed splashing onto our open mouths. Andrew caught the bulk of it but he was in a sharing mood, his lips coming back to mine, his tongue lapping into my mouth, bringing with it a generous helping of his husband's cum.

That bear certainly saw some things that night... and I finally had sex for the first time. I'll never forget it, and Bill and Andrew Thomas now have the babysitter that they have always dreamed about.

# CHAPTER 3
# TAKE ME

I'VE ALWAYS LOVED BEING a babysitter. I know that it's not exactly typical work for a young guy, but I don't have any desire to be a pizza delivery guy and I don't have the strength or motivation to work for my dad's construction company. There's a few parents who don't like a guy watching their kids, but most in my neighborhood are fine with it. Some even say that they're happier, that I'm less drama than a girl.

It's decent pay for not a lot of work, I typically look after kids who are old enough to not wake up in the middle of the night, but are too young to stay up past 9pm. I get to the house, I see them to bed, and I sit on the couch watching TV or reading a book. Knowing that I'm being paid to sit on my ass with free access to the fridge.

I sit for a few families in the neighborhood. Mostly the parents are friends of my parents, mostly they are really nice people who pay well and don't expect too much from me. One couple are very religious and have a house filled with pictures of Jesus. They're a little older than most parents, they have a son who was apparently a 'gift from god'. They are nice enough, pay well, but have nothing of interest in their house.

The Andersons though… they've got skeletons.

The Andersons live directly opposite from me. I've been sitting for them for a couple of years, after they moved into the neighborhood. One of the first things that I noticed about them was the way that Mr. Anderson always looks at me in a strange way, like he's undressing me with his eyes.

They have a pretty big house, the biggest on our road. We went over to their house when they moved in with a plate of cookies, welcoming them to the neighborhood. When my mom saw that they had kids, she offered my babysitting services. She's always pushed me, tried to get me out of our house and to make friends. I think she knows that I'm gay, but I think she's hoping it's a phase, that one day I'll meet a girl and settle down.

That night I was in my room, and was getting ready to go to bed. It was the middle of the summer and hot outside, I had my window open and my curtains drawn. The only house with a view of my bedroom window was the Anderson's, and I had been used to it being unoccupied for so long that I had forgotten that I might now be seen.

I stood in front of the window, as I often did, in my cotton briefs and short white t-shirt. My pajamas on hot nights, I don't have an AC in my room, just a big circular fan that brushes my skin when it passes. That night I faced the window and decided to change my top, bringing my shirt over my head, releasing my smooth and toned chest into the room.

I stood there, catching the sight of my reflection in the mirror by my window. I love to look at myself naked, to touch myself while I watch. I ran my bookishly slender fingers across my skin, caressing my nipples that instantly hardened at my touch. My short blonde hair danced in the glow of my bedside light as I stroked my flesh with my thumb and forefinger, my cock beginning to harden as I explored myself.

I dipped my hand into my boxers, still looking at myself in the mirror. My thick, meaty head so tender, so delicate as my fingernails ran along it. I felt my balls quiver as I touched them, sending a shiver down my spine as I circled my asshole with my thumb. My ass aching to be entered, my skin bristled as my fingers stroked my hard meat.

I took two steps backwards to lean on the edge of my bed, now fully framed in my open window as I arched my back, my chest lit by my bedside lamp. My fingers now buried inside my boxers, tugging at my foreskin. I gasped as I touched myself, rubbing my taint as I held onto my bedpost, biting my lip as I delved deeper and deeper into my little smooth ass. I felt my fingers becoming engulfed in my dark hole, my cock so hard as I rolled my head to one side, to look out of the window as I touched myself.

Suddenly, I jumped. Startled, afraid. In the house opposite from us, a figure stood in the window. The curtains fully drawn, a man stood, apparently staring right at me. He was tall, well built, and totally naked.

Even from this distance I could see that he was stroking himself. I could see that he was holding his cock in his hand while he watched me. I could see that his cock was massive.

I lunged for the window, pulling my curtains shut with a flourish. My heart pounded in my chest as I lay on my bed, totally still, only moving my arm to click off the light on my bedside table.

*'Who the fuck was that?'* I asked myself, my breathing shallow - my pulse racing. *'Who was watching me? Who was masturbating with me?'*

The next day, my questions were answered.

Mr. and Mrs. Anderson came to our house at around noon. It was a Saturday, and they told us that they had been invited to a party the next town over. My parents were clearly a little annoyed that these new neighbors apparently had a better social life than they did but they were all smiles and politeness for our new neighbors, and invited them into our house. I heard them talking from my bedroom, and went downstairs when my dad called to me.

As I hopped from the bottom step and walked down our hallway, I came face to face with the Andersons. She seemed nice enough, a little plain and frumpy. He was tall, well built and smiled at me knowingly.

*It was him! It was him who had been spying on me! It was him who had that massive cock in his hand!*

My heart picked up speed as they spoke, I hardly even comprehended any of the words. All that I remember was that I had said 'yes' when there was an uncomfortable pause, at which point Mrs. Anderson said that I should be at their house at 7pm. I had a job, I was going to watch their kids. In the house directly over the road from ours - in the house where hours earlier Mr. Anderson had stood, watching me touch myself.

I went to their house, on time, dressed in what I thought was a pretty sexy, but not overly so, outfit. I wore a smart pair of jeans, a black shirt with a couple of buttons left undone. I had showered and put gel into my hair - I had spent a lot of time making sure that I looked my best for my new employers.

Especially Mr. Anderson. He was attractive, for an older man. His hair had flecks of grey and he was slightly unshaven - but his blue eyes had danced as he had looked at me earlier. When he smiled he showed off some delightful dimples, and melted my heart a little. He seemed so mature, so professional, so nice. I had to remind myself in that moment that this was the same man who had been standing naked in the upstairs window, the evening before. His shirt was so clean, his suit so sharp. Tonight he was a world away from the man with the huge cock who had been staring at me while I touched myself.

The parents told me that their kids were in bed, and that I should just watch TV, help myself to anything that I wanted from the fridge, and to call them if there were any issues. As Mrs. Anderson went to the bathroom before leaving, Mr. Anderson and I were left alone in their hallway. He smiled at me, before leaning into my left ear. So close that I could smell his cologne, so close that I could feel his warm breath on my neck.

"I saw you last night" he said, sending a shiver through my body. "Did you see me?"

"Yes" I gasped, my cock hardening already as memories of the night before flooded my mind.

"Would you like to see more?" he said, leaning closer to me. His lips touched my neck as he spoke, a delicate kiss that made me his.

"Yes" I gasped again, totally in his control.

"Here's my cell phone number" he said, as he pressed a small piece of paper into my hand. "Text me at 9 PM" he whispered. "I'll take it from there."

I nodded, without saying a word. Mrs. Anderson came into the hallway to join her husband, who smiled at her before turning to me.

"Remember now!" he said, in a joyful tone. "If there's any issues, please let us know!"


I spent the next couple of hours in their living room, stepping over the still unpacked boxes to look at the family photos that had already been put onto their mantelpiece. They were a nice looking family, in each picture Mrs. Anderson seemed a little sad but Mr. Anderson beamed and held his children close to him. He was absolutely the head of this family, the man of the house. As the minutes slowly ticked away I found myself staring at my cell phone, waiting impatiently until the clock hit 9:30.

As soon as the display showed the time that I had been longing to see, I fired off my text. 'It's time' - I wrote. Seconds afterwards I heard the house phone ring, and rushed into the hallway to answer it.

"It's me", the rough voice of Mr. Anderson spoke. I held the receiver close to me, feeling my body aching for him. "I'll be there in 10 minutes. Go upstairs and find the room that I was in last night. Be naked."

My heart pounded as I hung up the phone. I felt so alive, so under his spell. I would do anything that he asked, and slowly stepped upstairs to the front room. Walking in I saw a single bed, a bedside table and the open window, facing my bedroom window opposite.

I felt so nervous as I stripped, baring my chest, my cock, my ass. God I wanted him, I couldn't hardly wait for him to show up. I removed my socks and touched my hard dick, sending a small wave of pleasure throughout my body as I waited. Sure enough, within ten minutes I saw headlight speed down the road and turn into the driveway, followed by the smalling of a car door.

I stood to face the wall, my back to the door as I heard footsteps traverse the stairs. I held my breath as he entered the room, a broad smile on his face as he inspected my body.

"You're good" he said, his pleasure apparent. "You're a good young man."

I turned, exposing my smooth chest to him. My nipples glistening in the moonlight of the room, my flat stomach aching to be touched. My cock, freshly shaven, twitching in anticipation. His eyes scanned my body, my chest, my face. Resting on my eyes he leaned closer to me, his hands moving slowly to my chest.

"I only have 30 minutes" he said, walking towards me.

"We'd better make the most of it then." I muttered, closing

my eyes and opening my mouth. I held my position for what felt like an age but what was actually less than a second, before feeling his lips upon mine.

His thick tongue darted inside my mouth, finding its partner quickly. We both exhaled emphatically, locked in the moment, breaking down the tensions that we'd both been holding for far too long. His strong hand grabbed my ass, his fingers clutching me close to him, my flesh convulsing at his touch. I ran my fingernails through his hair, holding him close to me as our tongues danced, his errant hand now sliding down my stomach, resting close to my belly button. I pushed him away from me, taking a look at this fine man.

"Too many clothes," I murmured, waving my hand in his direction. Cocking his head he smiled at me, winking as he took off his shirt. He bared his chest to me, his thick muscular form melting my heart and incresing my desire. Standing, so that his chest was close enough for me to touch him, he lowered his pants, allowing his thick, meaty cock to spring towards me.

At that point I was a virgin. I'd never seen another man's hard cock in person, not this close up, let alone touched, or tasted one. Within seconds I had accomplished both, grabbing his pulsating sword I leaned towards it, licking the head immediately. His hand slid down my belly, graduating towards my own thick, rapidly pulsating prick while I fed his cock into my mouth, feeling his veiny dick make its passage past my teeth - towards the back of my throat.

His fingers reached my ass, rubbing against me - instantly sending me into ecstasy. I pushed my hips forwards, grinding against him, allowing him to slide his middle finger into my willing canal.

This first human insertion into my asshole aside from my own hands sent me into a quivering frenzy as I sucked deeper on his cock, my hand now stroking his shaft as I begged for him to finger me deeper and harder. My ass pushed onto his hand, my hole gaping and contracting around him.

He increased his tempo, rapidly darting into my star with his hand, as I sucked deeply on his monster cock. He brought me close to orgasm while I gorged on him, now rock hard and starting to twitch in my mouth. As I rode on his hand he grabbed at my dick, the additional stimulus enough to send me over the edge. As I came on his fingers his dick jerked, before sending his hot cum down my throat. Dribbling out of the side of my mouth I caught it with my fingers, rubbing it into my chest.

I sat on the floor, gasping - allowing his salty cum to slide down my throat. I looked up at him to see that he was standing over me, still stroking his cock.

"You know" he said, "I think I want more. Do you think that's okay?"

I leapt to my feet, flinging my arms around him. Feeling his hard muscles, his cock against my stomach. I pulled my head back and stared at him, our eyes locked, our moment pure.

Without saying a word our mouths met, a mass of tongues and lips. His rough tongue danced with mine, my hair pushed from my face by his strong hands. I stood quivering as he touched me, his hands running up and down my body - finding targets, pushing buttons. His fingers pressed against my ass, my skin so incredibly smooth and responsive to his touch. Keeping my voice low I bit my lip as he ravished my chest, already wanting to moan I held onto my emotions, readying myself for my later commands.

His cock pressed into my stomach, pulsating, barking for my attention. Bending to meet his powerful tormentor, I kissed it gently, welcoming it back to my mouth. Even bigger than it had been before it throbbed in my hand, bobbing as I pressed my lips against it. I licked his shaft - the entire length - before sliding it into my mouth. His cock tasted so good, so manly. This first dick to have passed my lips was now playing with my tongue, pressing against the inside of my cheek. His balls in my view swung as he fucked my face, begging to be squeezed. Taking them in my hand I rolled them, pulling on them, teasing him, making him groan with pleasure.

Standing, Mr. Anderson turned me around and pushed my back, making me fall forward onto the bed with my ass in the air. At that moment I ached for him, my desire to feel his cock inside me immense. Turning to look at him I saw him staring into my eyes, into my soul, waiting for my instruction.

"Fuck me, Mr. Anderson," I whispered. "Fuck me now."

He turned, reaching for his wallet. I stared at him, making sure that my voice would be as imposing as possible.

"No condom." I ordered. "I need to feel you inside me."

My man needed no second invitation. Holding apart my ass cheeks he plowed his mighty sword into my gaping hole, burying it to the hilt. This first assault knocked the wind out of me, make me gasp and pant for air. His cock filled my tight ass so completely, so beautifully. Withdrawing he fucked me again, harder - deeper. His hands slapping my cheeks in rhythm he quickened his pace, rushing into me, stuffing every inch of my canal.

Harder and faster he fucked me, his balls slapping on my skin. I still knew that it was morally wrong, but it felt so fucking good. My arms and head swayed as he intensified, his cock steaming into me with such great power. As I rocked against the power of his movements I felt my orgasm overpowering me, a complete wave of pleasure consuming me whole, my cock splurting out onto the sheets below.

As I attempted to recover I felt him shudder as his orgasm approached, and felt him withdraw. Spinning and dropping to my knees I took his cock in my mouth once more, tasting my own strong scent on his meat. Strongly I sucked him, eager to taste him, anxious to not let him cum. With his hands on the back of my head he held me in position before groaning softly, his legs shaking as his orgasm began to arrive.

"I'm going to cum," he warned, breathless words spoken by a gratified man.

"No." I barked. "Cum inside me, Mr. Anderson."

I stood, then spread myself on the bed - my warm asshole focusing its attentions on his cock. I held my cheeks apart, inviting his approach. He leaned into me, holding his dick as it guided itself towards its target, pushing easily into my willing hole. I gasped once more as he pushed his way into me, his cock twitching as it entombed itself, his hips grinding on mine. He pounded into me, reaching his finish line as his tongue attacked my neck. I wrapped my legs around his ass as he pumped, not allowing a change of heart. As his back tensed he let out a throaty moan, his dick twitching inside me as he shot his hot cum inside me. As I felt the full force of his ecstasy I rocked against his impact, my own orgasm overcoming my helpless body.

He dressed quickly, and kissed me on the forehead before leaving the house. I still don't know exactly what he told Mrs. Anderson but they both arrived back at the house together, an hour later.

And that's where I am now, three months later. My mom still thinks that I'll grow out of being gay, that I'll find some girl that she can chat about babies and cross-stitch with. She's happy that I'm working more though, once or twice a week I'm at the Anderson's house, clearly they've seen something in my work that they like.

———

# CHAPTER 4
# HARD MEN INSIDE ME

I REALLY SHOULDN'T BE TELLING you about this…

I'm a good guy. I don't want you to get the wrong idea about me. I want you to know that I'm someone respected in the community – when anyone needs any odd jobs done around their place then it's me that they call on. Everyone knows that I'm gay, but that doesn't stop a lot of them from employing me to rake leaves, clean pools and babysit for their kids. The main thing in their eyes is that I work hard – they all support me, knowing that I'm 19 years old and that I'm going to college in the fall.

I want you to know that I work hard, I never drink, and that even though I came out of the closet two years ago, I've never had a serious boyfriend. I'm the kind of guy that people want to look after their kids – to look at me you might think that butter wouldn't melt in my mouth.

I don't want you to know that last week, I was fucked by two men – all while the children that I was supposed to be looking after were sleeping upstairs.

You might think that the parents of the kids would be mad if they had found out what I was doing – on all fours with one cock in my mouth and the other in my ass – before switching to take both cocks in my ass – fucked in a rhythmic motion that made me cum onto the floor below me. They might be pretty pissed if they'd known that I'd finished the evening being coated in the streaming cum of the two men – who stood over my naked and exhausted body, stroking their hard thick cock and showering my face with their sticky, hot cum.

You'd be half right. I bet the mom would be incredibly pissed if she had seen this scene. There's one pretty big reason why she would have been even more pissed than if these men were strangers…

But, one of the men was her husband. The father of the kids that were sleeping upstairs. The respectable member of the community.

The other man… well he was her boss.

It was just supposed to be a normal night. Mrs. John had called me earlier in the day to let me know that she had to work really late, an important deadline needed her attention. Her husband is a trader on the stock exchange, and he would be working from home but would be confined to his home office, on the phone with his colleagues in Japan all night. They needed me to put their kids to bed, and then stick around until she came home and could take over.

They paid me well. They're both successful people, in their own careers – and they have a beautiful and big house to show for it. They have lovely children, and they both drive new and expensive cars. They're pretty much a perfect couple, and I'm kinda jealous of them.

I live in a pretty run down house. My parents have split up, and I live with my mom and my younger sister. We are pretty poor, and we don't have a lot of nice things.

Whenever I babysit at the John household, I let myself daydream. Imagining that this is my house, with my kids and my car parked in the driveway. I imagine that I am a house-husband, and that I spend my days going for coffee dates with the rich women in the neighborhood. I imagine that my days are filled with fun activities, and that I go for massages, that we take awesome vacations together.

I imagine that I never worry about money.

I also imagine that Mr. John is my husband – and that when the kids are safely in bed, he pours me a glass of wine and then fucks me on the kitchen table. This is a fantasy that I thought was entirely based on complete fiction – I didn't think that Mr. John was in any way gay, I just created a gay profile for him in my mind and ran with it.

It's a fantasy that I've had for a while, if I'm honest with you. I'm not sure what came first – the desire for this life or the desire for this man – but it has got to the stage where I just didn't think I could handle myself around him anymore. I didn't trust myself alone in his presence – I didn't know what was going to happen.

Last week, a lot of things happened that should have happened.

I had got to their house pretty early – Mr. John had met me at the door and invited me in. I was always super friendly to him, and that night I wore some clothes that I wouldn't usually wear when I was going to their house – a very tight white t-shirt and a pair of very skinny jeans that showed pretty much everything that I was packing. I know that, because I could see that Mr. John was staring at me when I came into his house.

"Leo!" he said, a smile breaking out on his face as he saw me. His eyes were all over me, I could even feel his stare on my ass as I walked past him. "Good to see you. Very good to see you in fact."

"I know you'll be working tonight" I said with a smile, twirling my short brown hair playfully and chewing on a piece of gum – "If you get lonely up there though, you know where I am."

God, I'm such a flirt sometimes! I really didn't even know

what I was doing – there was no way that Mr. John would want anything to do with me! His wife is gorgeous – he's clearly got an eye for the ladies!

I put their kids to bed – they had been swimming in the backyard pool all day so they were plenty tired and fell asleep pretty quickly. Once that was done, I went downstairs and did what I usually did – grabbed a cold drink from their fridge and turned on their TV, hoping to find some kind of marathon that I could watch to tick away the hours. While I had obviously been flirting with Mr. John, and while I always held some kind of fantasy hope that he would come downstairs and declare his love for me or something, I was pretty sure that these scenarios existed only in my head and that nothing would ever actually happen.

I had turned on the monitor for the kids' room and had it placed on the coffee table in front of me while I laid on the couch and zoned out in front of the television. I was actually just letting my eyes drop to take a little nap, when I heard a giant roar from upstairs.

I was shaken out of my slumber. *What the fuck was that?* It didn't sound like it was coming from the kids' room – but what else could it be?

My questions were soon answered, as Mr. Carter flung open the door to his home office and came bounding down the stairs. He had a massive grin on his face, as though he had just won the lottery.

"Is everything okay?" I asked, standing and facing him. "I heard a noise – was it the kids?"

"Leo – everything is fucking awesome!" he shouted. "I just made a deal that is going to make me a LOT of money!" He bounded towards me, his arms outstretched. Maybe it's because my mind was still a little foggy from lying on the couch for so long and nearly going to sleep, but I instinctively held out my own arms too, meeting him in a warm embrace.

"Great work" I said, my arms stretching around his back.

Just feeling his body so close to mine made me feel so good – so comforted – so…

So fucking horny.

"Oh shit" he said, stepping away from me. "I'm sorry – I shouldn't use bad language in front of you." I noticed that his eyes weren't looking at my face, but at my groin. He was totally looking at my cock! I was still in a little bit of a fog from my nap, but as I saw where his eyes were drifting I looked down myself – noticing to my surprise that my dick was clearly hard, and straining against the fabric of my tight jeans.

"Oh Mr. John" I said, suddenly feeling as though I were actually living in that fantasy world that I had been creating for so long. "Please, I'm 19 years old now. I'm an adult. You can say anything you want to me."

"You're right" he said, smiling. His mouth opened slightly as his tongue started to slowly lick his bottom lip – his gaze still fixed on my groin. "I sometimes forget that you're legal."

"Legal?" I said, laughing. "Legal for what exactly?"

"You know what for" he said, his eyes finally coming to my own. "The wife isn't here, I've always liked you… and now, with this deal closing, I'm in the mood to fuck!"

Jesus. These words were music to my ears. Just hearing them from him, a man who I had always thought was totally straight, knowing that he wanted to fuck me, knowing that it could happen right here, right now… that turned me on so fucking much.

"Fuck me" I said softly. "Fuck me Mr. John – fuck me now!"

We rushed towards each other once more – my hands all over him – his rushing straight for my dick. Kneading my cock strongly through my clothing, I felt his body pressing against mine. He practically walked me backwards until my ass was jammed against the side of the couch – until I had no more room to back up any further.

"Leo" he gasped, his hands both still on my cock, rolling my balls – his mouth open, his desire for me so evident. "God Leo – I want to be inside of you."

I wanted the same thing. My fingers rushed to his belt buckle – running leather through metal quickly – unbuttoning him as his hands came to the bottom of my shirt. He lifted it quickly over my head – his thick fingers rushing to my twink nipples – twisting them strongly, making me bark in pleasure.

"FUCK!" I gasped, pulling his pants and boxers down over his ass – allowing his thick, hard cock to spring towards my hungry crotch. I let my head fly backwards as his head moved towards me, his thick wet tongue licking my neck – running up and down – grazing on my earlobe and sucking on my flesh. "Fucking HELL Mr. John – fuck me! Please! I need your fucking cock inside of me now!"

He dropped to his knees – unbuttoning my pants, sliding his fingers around my cock and pulling it towards him. I was already so hard, primed and ready for his mouth. With a look to my eyes he lowered his lips around the head of my dick and started to suck me.

I threw my head backwards, holding onto him with one hand as he licked my length, swirling his tongue around my fleshy head and sucking on me, his hand running for my balls – twisting them, stroking them as I fucked his mouth – driving my shaft deeper into his hot, wet mouth. God I loved this – I loved the feeling of Mr. John as he sucked on my cock – but something wasn't quite right. He was amazing, but he was just too far away from my ass. I needed him inside of me, I needed to feel his cock in my asshole.

"Now" I whispered, pulling his head away from my dick and holding it in my hands – looking deep into his soul. "Fuck me now Mr. John – break me open!"

He didn't even say anything – he just kind of nodded before wrapping his hands around my neck and pressing his thick cock against the entrance to my tight little asshole. He held it there for a few toxic seconds – letting the thick rubbery head of his weapon stroke the length of my cheeks – running up and down – teasing me, making me beg for him to fuck me.

I couldn't wait any longer… I needed to feel this cock inside of me. I licked my fingers and ran my hand down to his member – and wrapped my fingers around it, lubricating him – pulling him closer to me. Pressing his cock against my asshole – an asshole that was gaping and ready for him.

Suddenly, there was a noise. A noise that filled us both with fear – a noise that suddenly snapped us both out of this fantasy experience of ours.

It was the sound of the front door opening.

"FUCK!" Mr. John shouted – trying to pull away from me, but knowing just as I did that it was too late. The front door opened into the living room, there simply wasn't the time for us to escape. We both knew for sure that Mrs. John was about to walk into her living room to see her husband a nanosecond away from fucking the gay babysitter.

"Well well well!" a voice called out. That was strange, this wasn't a voice that I was familiar with at all. This certainly wasn't the voice of Mrs. John.

"Bob!" Mr. John called, spinning his head – his cock still standing guard at the entrance of my ass. "What the hell are you doing here?"

"Your wife asked me if I'd mind coming to the house to get her spare laptop" he said, stepping into my view. Bob was slightly older than Mr. John, but still cute in his own way. His eyes were fixed on us as he walked closer to us, a giant smile on his face. "Looks like it's a good job I said I'd do it for her, eh?"

"I guess that depends on if you're going to tell her" Mr. John said, his arms still wrapped around me.

"I guess that depends on if you guys want to let me join in", Bob said. At first I wondered if it were a joke, and I began to laugh – until I saw that they were both looking at me, waiting for an answer.

"Well Leo?" Mr. John said – his still hard cock still tantalizingly close to my gaping, puckering asshole. "What do you think?"

"I want your cock inside my ass" I said back to him. "I've wanted your cock inside my ass for so fucking long. I *need* it. I'd do anything for it. If that means sucking him off while you fuck me, then hell – get over here Bob, get that cock of yours in my mouth."

Bob practically skipped towards us – pulling his pants down as he ran, his hardening cock jumping for joy. Mr. John had the cock that I wanted – his was long and pretty thick – but this new cock? This was something else entirely. Bob's cock was fat – fucking fat! I didn't even know how I was going to get that cock in my mouth…

But I knew that I was going to try.

Mr. John seemed relieved, and seemed to be extra horny at the thought of fucking me while I sucked on the cock of his wife's boss. His hands moved to my flesh, one each grabbing onto my cheeks as he pulled them apart gently – before pushing his thick, hard cock deep inside of my willing ass.

"FUCK!" I groaned, feeling every inch of his length as it sped quickly into me – stretching my asshole wide open – sending a jolt of energy throughout my body. His balls slapping against me as he pulled out and rammed back into me – making my body shake, my cock sway beneath me as Bob came to the side of me – presenting his cock to my mouth. As Mr. John pummeled into me I leaned down – taking Bob's fat shaft in my hand – struggling to wrap my fingers even halfway around his massive thickness – this hard cock that was determined to fit inside of my mouth.

My body convulsed as Mr. John sped his cock deeper, faster inside of me – making a mess of my ass as I brought Bob's fat cock to my lips. My tongue extending to lick the helmet, running my spit all over him as my body made moaning sounds that seemed to come from deep within my soul. As he frantically fucked me, I lowered myself entirely – circling my tongue around him before taking him fully into my mouth.

"Yeah boy!" Bob called, his hands coming to the back of my head – pushing me down, making me gag on his massive cock. He gyrated his hips in time with the fucking that Mr. John was dealing out to my raw ass – face fucking me strongly as I gagged, slurped and sucked on his length. "Take it! Take it you little boy!"

My body felt so amazing, both men reaching around me to grab onto my hard cock, stroking me – squeezing my flesh – sending delicious shots of orgasmic pleasure throughout my ravaged body. I continued to suck on Bob, practically unhinging my jaw in an attempt to get his length inside my mouth – his fatness hitting the back of my throat as his hands tightened around my head.

"Holy fuck!" Mr. John yelled – his hand on my balls – squeezing me as his cock sped deeper and deeper inside my ravaged ass. "I'm going to fucking cum! Your twink ass is so fucking tight!"

This, wouldn't do. I needed more. I needed more from both of these men.

"Not yet" I ordered, holding my hand flat on his stomach, slowing his rhythm – making him wait. Not until I've felt both of your cocks in my ass. I want you two to DP me, okay?"

"Fuck yeah!" they both called in unison. Mr. John grabbing onto my legs, Bob taking my waist as they lifted me clean into the air and placed me gently on the floor. Bob came to stand over me, while Mr. John came to lie down on the carpet beside me. He leaned over to me, grabbing my shoulders and rolling me towards him until I lay on top of him – my ass in line with his cock.

"Fuck my ass!" I screamed – a volume that I would have never dared reach in this house before – not with the kids sleeping upstairs. "Fuck my ass, both of you!"

I felt his hands parting my ass cheeks as Bob came towards me, his thick juicy cock leading the way. My asshole already gaping – prepared by Mr. John as Bob knelt in front of me, his arms coming to my sides, his cock pressing against my raw hole, lining up alongside Mr. John's. As he began to inch his way into me, I felt Mr. John pushing his cock in time – both jostling for position inside my tight little ass.

I had never been double fucked in the ass before… I had thought that I would know what it felt like, but this was a feeling that I had not prepared myself for. Mr. John's cock already felt so fat in my ass – it felt as though it was filling me completely as he inched his way into my dark hole. I gasped, moaning with my mouth wide open – just as Bob forced his cock in as well – stretching me further.

"JESUS FUCKING CHRIST!" I screamed, as both men began to pummel into my tired, thin body. Sweat pouring off me as Mr. John withdrew, then plunged his cock deep into me once more. His balls slapping on my skin as he fucked my tight ass harder – Bob leaning over me, wrapping his hand around my cock and stroking me strongly as his fat dick sped into my orgasmic asshole. "FUCK! I'M CUMMING! FUCKING HELL I'M CUMMING!!"

Both men continued their fucking – moving in a rhythm that blew me away as I lay on the floor, doubly impaled by their thick cocks as they used and abused me – fucking me harder and stronger. Jesus, this was fucking heaven – and I knew that only one thing would top this all off.

"I'm gonna cum!" Bob shouted, his hand still stroking me as strongly as he fucked. "FUCK!"

"On me!" I called to both men. "Cum on my face, both of you!"

Bob first withdrew from my raw ass, standing up while

Mr. John extracted himself from me. He rolled and then stood next to the boss of his wife – both stroking their cocks as I lay on my back – rubbing my cock – my cum beginning to shoot from me as I felt a powerful wave of orgasm. My head leaning back, my eyes closed – my tongue outstretched.

"FUCKING HELL!" they seemed to both shout at the same time. Just as I opened my eyes to see what was happening, showers of their hot, sticky cum parachuted onto my body – coating my face, my eyes, my cock. As I rubbed my raw dick through the throws of my final orgasm – they both shot streams of their seed all over my hot, tired, sweaty body.

Bob was the first to leave… as soon as he had helped Mr. John to clean me up – taking great care and making sure that none of the cum spilled onto the carpet – he dressed, grabbed that spare laptop, and went back to Mrs. John.

Thankfully, I'm pretty sure that he won't tell her what happened at her home while she was working.

CHAPTER 5
# TAKE ME TONIGHT

I RUSHED home from school that day. That day, last week, I scurried home as fast as my legs could carry me, impatiently longing for my room, for my dildo, for my privacy.

My physics professor, Mr. Tanner, was at the front and center of my thoughts. He had asked me to stay behind after class to discuss a project of mine, he'd waited until the room was empty of all others before closing the door, turning the key to lock it.

"Just in case", he'd said - giving me a wink. My heart pounded inside my chest, my cheeks began to flush - was this the day I'd always dreamed about?

I've had a crush on Mr. Tanner since the moment I met him. He's young, probably mid 20's and he's not married, as far as I can tell. I don't know if he's gay or not but in my dreams he is, and he wants me. He's tall and slim but with strong arms, thick wrists. He's got short, curly brown hair and a wicked smile, a smile that cuts into my soul, warms my heart, hardens my cock. I've wanted to be held by him ever since, to feel his arms around me, to nuzzle into his chest, to take his cock in my mouth.

He moved closer, pulling up a chair next to me, joining me

at my desk. Our eyes met, his pupils dancing in the light, his devilish grin enchanting me.

"I wanted to talk to you" he said, his voice low - his gaze dropping to my chest. "It's a little personal though… is that okay?"

I could hardly believe my ears… was this really happening? I wanted to lean over to him, to grab him, to pull him closer to me. I knew that I had to play it cool though, there was still so much that could go wrong. What I wanted to do was wrong, I didn't want him to get into trouble, at least not unless he wanted to, of course.

"Absolutely" I said, trying to look at him but not lose myself in his deep blue, dreamy eyes.

"I don't want you to be embarrassed here" he said, looking down at his crossed arms, "but I thought you ought to know. Have you heard of the website ICaughtHimInThe-Act.com? It's where people can upload videos."

"I've never heard of it" I said, truthfully. "What is it? What kind of videos do people upload?"

Mr. Tanner looked embarrassed - shy. He started to sweat a little and shake as he spoke, clearly uncomfortable, clearly wishing he were somewhere else.

"They're porn videos" he said, after a long pause. His gaze now fixed on his shoes, he looked a shell of the man that I had fantasized about so often. "They're gay porn videos. Videos taken of guys who don't know that they are being filmed."

"Oh!" I said, now entirely not sure where this was going. "Why are you telling me this?"

Mr. Tanner stood, paced around the room and then came back to his chair. Still not looking at me, still clearly uncomfortable.

"I think you're on there" he said in a low voice. "I think I saw you on there. I can't be 100% sure because I couldn't see your face, but I'm pretty sure it was you."

I laughed. The only thing that I could think to do. I was embarrassed to all hell, but not as embarrassed as he clearly was. His face was bright red, his hands shaking. He had just admitted to me that he'd watched gay porn, and that he'd thought that he had recognized me for my body, not for my face.

"I doubt it" I said, entirely unsure of myself but eager to distance myself from what he thought he had seen. "My brother is the only person who knows how to even use a video camera in our house, and I don't think he'd do anything like that. Just out of curiosity.. what was the guy in the movie doing?"

Again Mr. Tanner looked to the floor - even more flustered than before.

"Masturbating" he said, bringing his eyes back to meet mine. "Masturbating and fucking himself with a black dildo."

As I left school my mind raced with a thousand thoughts. I may have managed to persuade Mr. Tanner that he hadn't seen me, but the evidence was there. I've owned a black dildo for a couple of months now, barely a night goes by when it isn't put to use. My brother has been really weird around me recently, and spends a lot of his time on the internet in his room. Last week I was checking through my wardrobe and found his camera in there, when I asked him about it he said that he was taking art photos out of my window and must have misplaced it in there. Looking back it was a crazy excuse but I trust him! Clearly misplaced trust, clearly he's been filming me.

And then there's Mr. Tanner. The man who I've desired for months, the man who teaches me. The man who I want. The man who admitted to me that he watches gay porn, and that he thought he was watching me.

He was watching me. He was watching me masturbate.

He saw me naked, on my bed, running my dildo along my body and across my cock. He saw me sliding my dildo into my gaping asshole, holding it inside myself, moaning, writhing, cumming. He was probably hard, watching me get myself off.

And that turned me right the fuck on.

I rushed home, barely stopping for traffic. I only had one thing on my mind - getting home, getting to my bedroom, getting naked and getting off. I ran upstairs to my room, threw my bag onto the floor, sped to my bedside table to get my trusted black dildo and lay on the bed.

My heart pounded as I pulled my shirt over my head. My pants soon followed, my cock jumping from my boxers, my fingers grabbing my flesh - twisting my nipples, my breathing already heightened by the rush home now mixing with gentle moans.

I ran the dildo across my dick, before allowing it to gravitate to my mouth. As I sucked on the plastic my free hand tugged at my boxers, loosening the fabric, allowing them to fall to the floor Standing in only my white cotton socks I had a moment of clarity, looking towards my wardrobe.

The door was ajar. From inside I could see a red light, blinking at me.

Ordinarily I would have been horrified, but today it turned me on. Knowing that I was being filmed, aware that Mr. Tanner might be watching this show soon. I decided to play it up for him, to let him know how much I wanted him to be with me.

"Oh god" I murmured, to myself but loud enough for the microphone to pick up my words. "Sir, please fuck me Sir, please fuck me Mr. Tanner Sir."

I lowered myself onto my bed, leaning backwards, giving the camera the best angle of my body. Baring my ass, fingering my hole. I kept the dildo in my mouth - sucking strongly - imagining Mr. Tanner's cock in its place as my fingers ran across my cheeks. My cock so hard, so large as I thought about him on top of me, lowering onto me, feeling his thick dick against my back. Widening my asshole with the fingers of one hand I lowered the dildo to my entrance, exhaling as I inched it into me, moaning as it stretched me.

"Oh yes!" I screamed, putting on a real show for the internet. "Fuck me Sir! I want to feel your cock inside me!"

I pushed the dildo fully into me, pressing the very end of the tool as far as it would go, feeling my ass expand to fit my toy, groaning as I writhed against the plastic cock that I was using to fuck myself with. Withdrawing it gently I could feel my scent upon it, bringing it again to my mouth I licked myself off the dildo, smacking my lips as I tasted my musk. My fingers again grabbing at my flesh I felt myself ready for more fucking, more cock. Bringing my companion to my ass again I slammed it into me, gasping, moaning, calling out the name of my professor.

"FUCK!" I gasped, breathless, sweat forming in the nape of my back as I fucked myself. Faster I pulled it out of me, more violently I slammed it back in. I held it in place as I wiggled my hips, inching it in as far as it would go, throwing my head back and stroknig my cock as orgasm approached.

"Oh yes!" I called, louder than I would have ever before dared. "Do me Mr. Tanner, cum inside me!"

I buckled on my bed as my furious wanking made me cum, my heart in my mouth as I rhythmically forced the dildo into my hungry ass. My body ravaged, my mind full of intoxicating hormones, my orgasm taking over my being. I called his name repeatedly, summoning him, speaking directly to him, hoping to god that he'd come with me.

After I came I dressed quickly and went down the hall to my brother's room. I didn't want to let him know that I knew, but I wanted to give him the opportunity to get this video online as soon as possible. I was still a little mad at him, but still incredibly turned on that among the thousands of horny men that might see me naked, one was the one that I wanted. I told him that I was going to be going out for a while, and that I'd call him when I needed a ride home. Simple, gave him the all clear, part two of my plan was coming into shape.

When I woke the next morning I wondered if I should check the website - see if my body was on show for the masses. My brother has a computer in his room and I use the family one in the living room for my homework. I didn't want to ask my brother to use his, he's very protective of his computer - and now I know why. Using the one in full view of the kitchen was probably a bad idea too, even if I weren't caught I'd probably leave traces of my activity all over it. I'm way too clueless when it comes to computers, I figured that my best course of faction was to carry on as normal. Besides, I had a class with Mr. Tanner that morning.

Mr. Tanner was a little late for class. I was worried at first, thinking that I had made a huge mistake. A few minutes past the hour he appeared, looking a little the worse for wear. Looking like he hadn't slept at all.

Class proceeded as normal. Mr. Tanner seemed a little distracted - I noticed that he didn't really look at me. I did catch him though, during a time when he had us writing from the board I looked up sharply to my left to see him, standing in the far corner of the room, staring at me. His glance shifted as soon as I put my eyes on him, clearly guilty, clearly caught.

When class was dismissed I packed my things into my bag slowly. As everyone else left I wandered to the door, eager to be the last to leave. Just as I was about to exit I heard his voice, shaken - nervous.

"Um… Simon? Could you… um… see me for a minute?"

Bingo.

I had prepared for this part of the lesson. Practiced. I knew that Mr. Tanner would need me to hold his hand, to lead him. I turned, faced him and smiled, before walking with strong, masculine towards his desk.

"I wanted to talk to you too, actually" I said in as confident a voice as I could muster.

"Oh really?" he said, seemingly taken aback by my fortitude. He seemed to relax in front of my eyes, to gain in stature. His dimples returned to his cheeks for the first time today as a smile broke out across his face.

"Uh huh" I said coyly. "You see, I was… um… working on something last night. I was wondering if you could help me with it?"

"Oh you were, huh?" he said, his hand on his hips. His eyes ran along the length of my body, my outfit picked out especially for him. A white t-shirt with an open neck, plenty of chest hair on show. A pair of tight fitting stonewash jeans, and my trusted scruffy sneakers. I looked, if I may say so myself, delicious - and the bulge that was appearing to grow in Mr. Tanner's pants told me that I wasn't alone in my analysis.

"Mmmm" I said, running my finger across my chest. "You see, I was working really HARD at something, but I think I need you to give me a hand. You catch my drift?"

"I think I know what you were working on" he said, standing with his legs apart. "I think I may have seen you."

"I think you may have" I said, raising my eyebrows at him. "I was thinking, seeing as you're an expert - and a teacher of course - maybe you could teach me how to do it better?"

"What would you like me to teach you?" he asked with a hushed voice. He took a step closer to me, his hands in front of his groin, covering his stiffness. I turned, facing his desk. I felt him come behind me, just inches away - I could feel his breath on my neck as I turned to face him.

"Everything" I whispered, as I bent over his desk. "Teach me everything."

He came up behind me like a shot, his hands on my jeans, his manly fingers clawing at the fabric, pinching my flesh beneath. I gasped as he roughly reached around my waist to unbutton me and pull my pants over my moons, as he took control, as he dug his nails into my ass - kneading me, making me so fucking hard as he made me his. My chest scraped across his desk sending papers flying as he ruggedly massaged my buttocks, my cock now rock solid, my ass yearning to be made his.

His fingers reached my groin, grabbing onto my stiffness, his grip jerking my dick. I groaned as he touched me, my ass gaping, my desire for him to the max as he teased me, gently then hard, flicking my button, sending me wild. I widened my stance, my shoes dragging on the floor as I opened myself up for him.

I heard him behind me, breathing heavily, his fingers dipping into my asshole. I heard him unzip his pants and his belt hit the floor, followed by his knees. His hands still on my ass parted my cheeks, I jumped as his thick, coarse tongue hit my hole. I felt his nose press against me as his tongue delved deep into my ass, my cock so hard as he ate me out, his fingers parting my cheeks to offer further access.

I gasped, grabbing the edge of my desk - my knuckles white as I held on. My ass pressing against his face I pushed back further onto him, his wet tongue delivering charges of passion into my asshole, his hand reaching through my lips to stroke my cock- sending me close to orgasm. I bucked on his desk, reaching to grab his head as he continued to fuck me with his tongue - my legs shaking as held on for dear life, my cock ready to explode, my ass ready for him.

"Fuck me!" I called breathlessly. "Mr. Tanner please! Fuck me!"

He stood behind me, holding my ass apart. I couldn't see

but could feel his thickness against the entrance to my hole, looking forward, bracing myself. He held his cock against my ass while he shifted his position, moving his hands to my shoulders. Grabbing onto me he applied his pressure, forcing his dick into me.

I gasped as he entered, his thick cock stretching my tunnel wide, his girth making me moan, quiver, shake. His manhood filled me completely with inches to spare, his powerful thrusts coursing through me. He groaned as he pumped his giant cock into me, his balls slapping on my ass as he increased his rhythm, his hands moving from my shoulders to my cock – masturbating me furiously with his thick fingers as he fucked me, grabbing onto my flesh as he powered into me.

I lifted myself slightly from the desk as he fucked, giving him greater access to my dick, reaching my hand around my neck to grab onto his head, pulling him closer, feeling his breath and his tongue on my neck. His wonderful thrusting, his powerful pumping of my defenseless ass sending me close to orgasm. His firm ass clenching as he fucked me, my sweat pouring down my neck. I reached around with my free hand to grasp his head - now held with both hands - as I came, shaking uncontrollably, screaming as I came on his desk - my ass grabbing onto his dick as I felt the most powerful orgasm take over my body.

I released my tight grip on his head and collapsed to the desk once more, quivering as the waves of orgasm escaped. I slid from the desk and fell to me knees, spent. Turning I came face to face with Mr. Tanner's hard cock, waving itself in my direction. Without a second thought I lurched forwards, grabbing onto his shaft, taking him into my mouth.

His taste overpowering, his scent mixed with mine. This monster cock in my mouth felt so wonderful, I sucked hard onto his head and tickled his balls with my nails. My tongue running the length of his thickness, my lips wrapping around his helmet, my throat feeling the tip of his cock as I fed him into my mouth. I sucked hard on him, stroking his cock with my hand as I slurped on his dick, milking him.

He started to shake as I worked his cock, his hands on the back of my head as his might started to twitch inside my mouth. His grip increased as he pushed my face onto him, his balls tightening as he released his hot cum into my mouth.

We dressed quickly, aware that the room would soon be filled with students. The air smelled like sex but there wasn't too much that we could do about that, we shared only glances, no words as we gathered our belongings.

In the corridor we walked together, each quickly trying to get to our next rooms. At the water cooler he motioned that he was turning left, whereas I was going right.

"Thank you Mr. Tanner" I said, my voice still a little shaky. "I think you've taught me a lot."

"You're welcome Simon" he said, giving me a wink. "I spent a lot of time online last night researching. I'm glad it could be useful."

———

# CHAPTER 6
# GLORY

"A JOB IS A JOB" my mom kept saying to me. "A job pays you money which pays me rent. Okay?"

I didn't want a job, but apparently I needed one. The thought made me sick to my stomach, I didn't want to get up every day to go somewhere that I didn't want to go. I didn't want to have to report at a certain time to a certain person and fake smile at customers or colleagues. All that I wanted to do was to sit at home and play video games, chat online, and put various household objects into my ass while I dreamed about being fucked by dirty men in back alleys. A job gets in the way of that.

"Here" mom said. "Take the paper, search the jobs, go on an interview, get a fucking job."

I huffed, and snatched the paper from her hands. She knew as well as I did that no-one places ads in print anymore, she also knew as well as I did that if I started to look for a job online I'd be quickly distracted by something else. Within five minutes I'd be watching a video clip of a guy with a 10 inch dick fucking some skinny white boy in the ass before cumming on his chest. I'd have my fingers on my cock before the movie stopped buffering, I'd shake the floor below me before the guy even had a chance to rip off his shirt and throw him onto the bed.

I'm obsessed with porn and with getting myself off. I had a boyfriend, but he moved away to college a few months ago and I haven't been motivated enough to put myself out there. I game, I watch porn, I masturbate, I sleep. That's been my life, and I've loved it.

But mom is right. I do need a job. I just don't want one.

The newspaper was full of the usual. Assistant at a car wash. Ugh. Filing clerk at a law firm. Double ugh. Stock replenishment at a supermarket. Give me a fucking break. Cashier at an adult store. Hello!

I grabbed the paper and ran downstairs. Throwing on my shoes I called to my mom, letting her know that I was on my way to see a man about a job. I quickly jumped into my car, and sped towards the adult store.

I was pretty much hired on the spot. I walked into the store and immediately caught the attention of the manager who was filling in on the cash desk. I was wearing a short red shirt that showed my belly button and cut off jeans with my Dockers. I've always been able to spot a gay guy and zeroed in on him as I lent on the counter, twirling my long brown hair as I asked him if his position was still vacant. His gulp and bulge in his pants told me that I was just the candidate that he was looking for, and he reached behind himself to grab the 'Help Wanted' sign out of the window. The job, was mine.

I spent most of the first day learning the ropes and checking out the customers. They were mostly men, there were a few couples, and most bought DVD's and dildos. To the back of the store was a curtain, and when I was relieved from my shift by Donna, I asked her what was down there.

"Booths" she said, with a wink. "The customers can go there and watch movies. $1 buys them 10 minutes."

"Shit!" I said. "People will do that? In the store?"

"Oh, they'll do much more than that" Donna said with a sly smile. "Why don't you go on down there and check it out for yourself?"

I had nothing to do for the rest of the day, and I liked the store. These were my kind of people, I enjoyed being there and didn't think of my time there as 'working'. If I were stacking shelves at the supermarket I would have been long gone, but this place felt good.

And, I wanted to know what was going on at the back of the store.

I walked towards the back, conscious that there were about 20 guys who were looking at me. The clearly gay ones had all tried to flirt with me at the counter - all were nervous and clearly aroused. Now I was one of them, a customer.

At the back of the store there was a small red curtain. To the side a sign, telling people that the booths were down the hallway. I pushed the curtain aside and walked, turning once, before seeing the booths.

There were 8 in total, 4 on each side. Each totally self contained with a door not unlike a public restroom toilet. Three of the doors on each side were closed and apparently occupied, one at the far end of the row on the right was vacant, one in the middle of the row on the left. Choosing the closest door to me, that on the left, I scurried into the booth and closed the door behind me.

The previous occupant had clearly finished before his money had. The video was still playing and there was a musky scent of sweat and cum in the air.

In the middle of this darkened room there was a wooden stool, low to the ground. The screen filled one wall and showed a girl being fucked in the ass by one guy while sucking on the cock of another. Her moans filled the room, the closed space combined with the smells and sounds turned me on greatly. I'm not typically a fan of straight sex but there was something about this movie and this booth that did something to me. As I lowered myself to sit on the stool I realized that my cock were already becoming hard - my ears pricked as I listened to the sounds of this girl's tight little ass being rammed by the huge pink cock of her partner.

I couldn't take my eyes off the screen as I saw her gag on the black cock in front of her, both men had a hand on the back of her head and were forcing her to choke on this thick piece of meat. Her tits seemed ravaged, already sucked and flicked - her nipples stood firm as she scraped on the bed towards this dick in her mouth. Her tongue flicked around his balls as she deep throated him, the force from the ass fucking making her lurch onto his thickness even further. As my own ass hit the cold wood of the stool I jumped slightly, gasping audibly as I continued to stare at the screen.

My own cock began to beg for my touch as I watched, the fingers of my right hand naturally gravitating towards my stiffness. I ran my digits past my chest, stopping only to roll my hard nipples through my shirt as I sped towards my lurching dick. While I watched this girl getting hard fucked I felt so turned on, so horny, so needy for a cock to suck and a dick to fill my ass.

I reached my fingers towards my cock, running them along my pubes, flicking my helmet. My breathing quickened, my shallow moans increased in volume as the sounds of fucking from the video filled the tiny room. My fingertips dipped closer to my ass as I continued to watch this girl, my balls so tender to my touch, my knees knocking, making the stool that I was now precariously balanced upon wobble. My left hand flew towards the wall beside me, grabbing onto a hole in the wood, allowing me to steady myself.

I turned my head to see where my hand was gripping. A fairly large hole, carefully cut into the wall. I looked to the other side to see a mirroring cut. Two holes, both apparently a keyhole into the booths beyond. *What the fuck is this?*

I moved closer to the hole to my left, peering through to

see a video playing in the booth next to me. It was too dark to see the occupant of the room, but the sounds of heavy breathing allowed me the knowledge that it was occupied. As I moved closer to the hole, my mouth open in wonderment, a shadow fell across the opening.

I crept backwards, figuring that I had been caught peeping on my neighbor. Just as I considered running from the booths a thick, hard cock appeared, pushing through the hole, bending towards me.

*A GLORYHOLE!* I thought to myself. I had heard of them but had never considered that the adult bookstore had them. The idea had always seemed so dirty, so strange. Yet here I was, in a gloryhole, with a cock pointed towards me.

My mouth gaped as I saw this proud dick and as my mind raced to its conclusion. In the light of day I was sure that I would be disgusted by the idea, but there was something so carnal, so hot about this that turned me on so much. This was pure filth. This was just sex, nothing else. I had no idea who this man was, what he looked like, how old he was, anything about him. All I knew was that his cock was hard and that he wanted to use my mouth. And God did I want him to use my mouth.

I leaned towards him, getting a closer look at this bobbing dick. He was rock hard and had a thick, meaty dick, uncut and proud. I reached my hand towards him, stroking him gently, my mind racing as I considered what I was about to do. Without a word passing between us, I leaned forward to take him in my mouth.

He tasted so strong, so sweaty, so good. I ran my tongue along his shaft while cupping his balls through the hole, sucking on his head, peeling back his foreskin to taste him. I sucked strongly on him, forcing his cock to the back of my throat where his thickness played with my tonsils, my spit coating him, my lips wrapping around him, my hair dropping to tickle his length. I felt so incredibly turned on as he face fucked me, my cock hardening, my desire increasing.

I dropped my hand to my cock, playing with my flesh and pressing against my taint as I continued to suck. This stranger, this man who I knew nothing about slid his thick dick down my throat as I dipped my fingers into my ass. I squatted on the floor closer to him, trying to get more of him inside my hungry mouth as he rocked against the partition. Pulling him away from my mouth so that I could catch my breath I looked behind me, spotting that there was now a hand reaching into my booth through the hole in the opposite wall.

This new entry reached towards me, trying to touch me. I stood and bent over, still with a hand on the first cock but with my ass pointed towards the hand, allowing him to touch me. His fingers grabbed my moons and quickly moved to my ass, diving into my dark tunnel as I brought my mouth back to the cock of the first man.

Here I stood, with my mouth on dick and my ass in the air, getting fingered by this second man. His fingers slid easily into my hole as I moaned with pleasure, my throat filled with the meat of my initial stranger. The hand behind me started to spank me, grabbing at my ass, pulling me towards him. As I looked around I saw that he was holding something, something small. Something shiny, something scandalous.

This new man was offering me a condom.

My heart now pounding, my inhibitions long since flown. I span around to grab the condom and ripped it open quickly, not even giving this man chance to stand and put his cock through the hole before I was ready for him. As he placed his dick inside my hovel I stopped to admire its length, its thickness, its proud erection. Leaving my first cock for a moment I spat on this new monster, rubbing my saliva into his flesh and wrapping my fingers around him, stroking him furiously.

I took the condom in my teeth and placed my lips onto his

thickness, rolling the sheath down his length. *His cock was huge!* So thick, so long. Under normal circumstances I might be afraid to let this beast anywhere near my ass, but these were not normal circumstances. My mouth had already been stretched by two cocks, my ass wanted in on the action as well.

I turned, my back to the wall and felt between my legs for this dick. This unit that was about to enter into me, this man who I had never met before and would probably never meet again. I bent over, allowing my asshole to see his cock, then pulled him towards me. The uncomfortable position only heightening my desire for him, I kept my eyes on the dick in front of me which waited for my mouth. Pressing the thickness against my star I bent over more, allowing him to slip inside.

I gasped as he entered, a couple of exploratory strokes until he was sure that he had reached his target, followed by stronger strokes into my willing hole. I leaned forward, making sure to keep this dick in my back passage, to grab hold of the dick that my mouth still yearned to suck.

My mouth fell onto his sword, sucking him strongly as the thick cock of the man behind me continued to pump into me. I bounced my ass backwards to fuck him as I sucked again on the other mans cock, slurping on his shaft and grabbing onto his balls as my knees shook with the force of the walled fucking. Faster and stronger he pounded into me as my tongue wrapped around the cock in front of me, my mouth dripping saliva onto the floor beneath me, my neck bulging as the cock slid down me, my cock ready to burst as my very being shook against the double ended assault of my strangers. I grabbed ahold of the opening that framed the dick of the first man as my orgasm approached, shuddering throughout my every fiber as I slammed my ass onto the thickness of stranger number two, while the cock in my mouth began to twitch and to give up its strength.

I pulled him away from my mouth as he came, shots of his hot cum streaming onto my face and up my nose. His salty escape combining with his deep groans turning me on further, I shook as wave upon wave of orgasm caused my ass to grip the dick that plundered it, I screamed as my pleasure increased. Still holding onto the cock of the first man I increased my tempo, pounding my ass onto the wall and allowing the dick that pierced it to reach further into my raw ass - my poor raw asshole which now seemed unable to take any more abuse at the hands of this monstrous stick. I groaned loudly as I came again and again, sending my seed to the carpet below and onto the wall in front of me as I rolling my stiff nipples with my fingers, as I shook violently under the pressure of multiple orgasms. As I lurched forwards I felt his cock escape from the clutches of my tight ass- before hearing the snap of latex as his condom was removed. Still bent over, sweat pouring from every pore of my body, I felt his hot cum splatter on my ass and my back - each drop sending me again to the point of ecstasy. Turning and dropping to the floor I scooped cum from my back and my ass and brought it to my neck and my mouth, tasting both men and rubbing their seed into my chest.

I must have stayed in that booth for a while, collecting my senses and my thoughts. Every now and then a cock would appear at the hole, but I had to politely refuse. My exhaustion took over, I knew that I had to leave.

I also knew that I would return.

---

# CHAPTER 7
# WATCHING THEM

MY LIFE IS a whirlwind of secrets…

The first secret is my own. I'm gay, and I haven't told anyone. Everyone thinks that I'm straight, and that I'm just being a hardworking guy who doesn't have time to date girls right now. I'm 21 already but I'm going to college in the fall, and it's there that I intend to really come out and find a guy.

That was the plan, at least. What really happened is that I saw my next door neighbor plowing a guy that he'd met online, and then spent my first gay night with him after he caught me watching them.

It all happened last week. I have a good relationship with my next door neighbor, and he has a backyard pool that he lets me use. I spend a lot of time over there and we chat about a lot of things, I really thought that we were pretty good friends.

The only weird thing is that he thought that I was totally straight, and I thought that he was too!

He pretty much lets me use his pool whenever he wants. I know where the spare key to his house is kept, and I'm totally allowed to let myself in, use his bathroom - make a sandwich or get myself a drink. Whatever goes, and I'm there quite often. I sometimes give him a heads up that I'll be over, I sometimes just show up. And, that's what happened the other week.

I had gone over to his house after my shift at the supermarket. The last time that i'd spoken to Greg, I'd said something about not coming over that night so he could have reasonably expected to have some privacy. I guess that I should have at least texted him, but to be honest it totally slipped my mind.

I guess that it didn't slip his mind. When I got to his house I was going up the stairs to take a quick shower in his bathroom - as I usually did before getting in his pool, when I heard the unmistakable sounds of fucking.

Gay fucking.

Gay fucking with Greg, my sexy next door neighbor.

'Oh God' he called - clearly unaware that I was in the house - 'fuck me - harder! Fuck me harder and give me your fucking cum!'

I was standing close to the top of the stairs when I heard it... and those words made me become rooted to the spot. They were coming from his bedroom, which was now just a few feet from my position. Looking towards that room, I saw that his door was open.

The headboard was hitting the wall, making a noise that sounded as loud to me as my own heart beat. I was so excited to hear this, and so fucking turned on! I didn't know if it was the beer, or because I knew that Greg was naked and hard in there; but I simply had to get closer to the action - I had to see his cock, I had to get some idea of what it would be like to be fucked by him. I had to see what was going on in there!

I knew that I should respect their privacy and go to the bathroom, or just exit the house altogether and go home - but I also knew that my desire wouldn't ever forgive me if I did. I kicked off my shoes and crept across the hallway towards the door to that exciting bedroom, noticing that the bedside lamp was on and that they were on the bed - some guy that I had never seen before kneeling on all fours with Greg behind him - his ass facing me.

Damn, as soon as I saw them my cock began to harden - my heart rate increased and a shower of goosebumps crept across my body. I could feel my asshole puckering as I spied on them, seeing Gary with one hand on his back, the other in the air - his palm open and beginning a fast descent onto the stranger's plump ass.

THWACK!

'Fuck!' the man barked, his skin flushed. As Greg raised his hand once more I could see the entire outline of his hand, all five fingers in a red mark on that fine looking ass. I jumped as he hit him, my legs weak - my cock growing so hard as I slowly ran my hand down my body, watching them fucking. Greg's hand flew down onto his partner again - shifting him further down the bed as he spanked him - his free hand coming from behind his back to slide underneath her body - sweeping him up until his arms were off the bed. He held his new friend like this, his hand running across his chest and then dropping to his groin - holding onto his hard cock as he stroked his shaft - just as my own fingers were stroking mine through my shorts.

Greg's swinging balls told the tale of his cock as it held itself deep inside of his new partner - as one of my hands held onto the outline of my cock through my thin shorts while the other slid toward my ass cheeks. I knew that I was risking a lot by even being here, but I had to see more, I had to match the actions with the noises that were coming out of that room. As they shifted positions, as my next door neighbor's friend fell forwards and motioned for him to lie on the bed - my hand slipped into the band of my shorts, pulling my briefs to one side so that I could slide my digits along the sensitive shaft of my hard, throbbing cock.

I braced myself against the door opening, knowing that I

could be caught at any second but really not giving a fuck as my next door neighbors fuck partner climbed onto Greg - holding his cock beneath him and sinking onto him, sliding his girth deep into his gaping asshole. Greg's hands rushed to his partner to grab at his flowing, hard cock, squeezing his flesh and stroking him roughly as they both rose and fell, the seyx stranger riding him - his head flying back as Greg picked his up from the bed and opened his mouth to lick the tip of his man's cock. Greg's hands wrapped around his waist as he filled his asshole with that hot, hard cock - Greg's mouth latched onto a hard cock as they sucked and fucked.

My god, I don't know if it was watching this, hearing them moaning, or smelling their scent as the friend rode Greg close to an orgasm that was affecting me the most, but as soon as the tips of my fingers brushed against my asshole, I almost came myself. My legs buckled as my fingers dipped deep inside of my tight, hot hole - as my neighbor's friend took a pounding, riding Greg strongly while he sucked on his helmet. Fucking hell this was so sexy, so hot - I had to stroke myself harder and take myself over the edge. My left hand grabbed at my ass cheeks, pulling my shorts down past my knees to grab at my dark hole - rubbing myself and making myself so turned on - my neighbor's friend lifting himself up and sinking on that fat cock, their moans now just a soundtrack to my own pleasure. I wasn't even watching them as I came, my cock exploding, my cum streaming onto my fingers as my legs shook uncontrollably, as I had the most powerful orgasm ever, timed apparently with theirs as they both groaned loudly - louder than I would ever dare. As my body and mind began to come down from this amazing experience I picked up my head, seeing that my neighbor's friend had collapsed on Greg's chest - his back heaving as he struggled to catch his breath. As I scanned them both, my gaze rested on Greg's, seeing that his eyes were as wide open as mine - and that he was staring right at me.

Fuck.

I'd been caught, the man who I secretly desired had seen me, with one hand on my cock and the other reaching for my asshole, with my cum on my fingers and a guilty as sin look on my face. We shared a look at each other in complete silence for a good few seconds, before I suddenly snapped out of it and tiptoed quietly away towards the stairs.

That all happened on the Tuesday of last week. I felt very guilty, and I didn't swim in the pool, but I just went home and went up to my room. I felt horny, sure - and I replayed the events of what I had seen over and over in my mind, but as much as it all turned me on *so much* - it also worried me. I was concerned that greg wouldn't want to talk to me again, and that he wouldn't want me to come over to his place anymore. As much as I considered that, I realized that it wasn't his pool that I was going to miss - it was him. I really didn't want to stop talking with him, gently flirting with him - and watching him in his tight swim trunks. The thought of not going over there was making me pretty sad, and that carried over until the Wednesday - up until I got a surprise text message on my cell phone, from Greg.

'Hey man' he said. 'Wanna come over? Maybe swim - maybe...'

'Maybe....?' I responded, keeping things cool, not wanting to push things even though my heart was beating in my chest.

'Maybe - you know' he replied, coyly. 'Maybe fool around a bit?'

I was at his door before the returning text message had even successfully sent.

'Hi sexy man' he said, opening his front door to greet me with a smile. 'Come in'.

'I've been naughty' I said, turning to speak to him after I entered into his home. I was remembering the previous night, and the way that Greg had spanked his friend. I hoped that he would take the bait, that he would know which direction I was trying to take this. Thankfully, he wanted this to go the same way that I did.

'You've been very naughty indeed' he said, smiling a little, and licking his lips. 'What should I do to you?'

'I don't really know...' I said, coyly. 'What would you like to do to me? I am such a naughty little fucker...'

'Well' he said - suddenly looking a little more stern. 'If you don't get upstairs right now... into my room, and take those clothes off - I'll spank you!'

Holy fucking hell, those toxic words turned me on so much!

'I've got a better idea' I said, standing on the stair with my hands on my hips, 'How about I go to your room and take my clothes off... and *then* you spank me?'

He rushed towards me, quickly - grabbing onto my waist and spinning me around, bending me over at the same time. My palms hit a stair as my legs widened, my sneakers making it uncomfortable for me to brace myself as his hand rushed up my legs pawing at me, brushing against my sensitive inner thighs as he pulled at my short shorts, pulling them down over my ass cheeks to allow access to my hot asshole and my hard cock. His hands were all over me, rubbing my cheeks, smoothing them, rubbing them with his palms and pulling my underpants fully over my ass. God I wanted him right there and then - I wanted him to pull out his cock and push it into my...

THWACK!

'FUCK!' I screamed, feeling a volley of pain rushing through me. My ass tingled, hot and red with this slap. 'FUCKING HELL! THAT HURT! DO IT AGAIN!'

THWACK!

Another - another hit on my ass that made such a satisfying sound, my ears ringing as my cheeks slapped together - my cock fucking pulsating as his fingers pressed hard against my puckering ass, sending my face to the edge of the step as he began to roughly finger fuck me. At this rate we weren't even going to make it up to his room - but a promise was a promise, and I still wanted to show him my naked body, I still wanted him to suck on my cock and fuck me until he came inside of me!

I scampered up the stairs, on all fours as his fingers breached inside of my asshole and remained inside of me, leading me like I was his puppet. I could feel each one, each finger twisting and turning inside of me - wrestling with my heat and my hormones. My mouth open, moans escaping as I scrambled up the stairs, finally able to stand straight and rush into his room.

Gary followed me quickly, ripping off his clothes as he walked, dropping them on the floor behind him until he stood in front of me, the backs of my legs pressed against the side of his mattress as he fell towards me. His strong hands reached for my shirt, ripping it over my head quickly, before dropping to his knees to pull my clothing away from my legs until he was face to face with my hard cock. He stood for a second, his hands reaching for my hardness, his eyes trained on me while he was licking his lips. I couldn't wait - I just had to have his mouth on my sensitive dick.

'Suck me' I begged, as I brought my hands to the back of his head. 'Suck on my cock - it's all yours now!'

His mouth flew towards me - his tongue lapping around my helmet, his lips closing around my erect shaft as he sucked strongly. My body felt weak as he sucked on me - his lips latching onto me as his fingers crossed from one bouncing ball to another. His hands wrapped around my back and slowly dropped to my ass - his strong fingers grabbing onto my flesh and squeezing me, pulling my cheeks apart so that he could delve those digits into my hot asshole. He was opening me up, all the while sucking on my cock as he dipped into me, rubbing my opening and finger fucking me as he grunted at my cock.

'Fuck me' I begged him, stroking his hair as he sucked on me, bringing me to the edge of an orgasm. 'Please Greg, give me your cock - fuck me!'

Like he needed to be asked twice...

His trembling hand went straight from my asshole to his pants, quickly stepping out of his clothing and bringing his cock into the room. My eyes dropped to see the monster that was just about to impale me, my eyes grew bigger as I saw what was coming. That cock was so long, and so fucking meaty - so hard and so ready, with veins pulsating and a shaft that was darting straight towards my ass.

'Oh FUCK!' he groaned, as he widened my legs, sitting my ass onto the bed - and widening my legs. His lips quickly darted from my chest to my mouth, his thick hot tongue flicking mine and then back to my nipples - lapping at me as he pressed that fat cock at the entrance to my opening.

'DO IT' I said, staring into his eyes as he held the head of his cock at the entrance of my asshole. My dick stood to attention as he looked back at me, a curious mixture of guilt, pleasure, and desire on his face. I know that he was thinking about my parents who he is good friends with, but here he was - standing at the entrance of their son's naked ass - about to enter into his tight little hole. 'Do it - fuck me Greg take me! Fuck me until you cum deep inside of me!'

As he threw that hard cock into me I collapsed back onto the bedsheets, feeling every single inch of that dick as it speared into me, filling me totally, stretching me wide open as he buried himself. God his cock felt so good, so powerful as he withdrew - leaving me gasping, begging for him to come into me again. His back arched as his body fell towards mine, his ass raising and falling as he slammed that dick so deep - hitting the very back of my asshole, sending my cock into overdrive, my cum getting so close to spilling as he withdrew and came back - fucking me so hard - making me yelp with excitement and pleasure. 'FUCK!' I gasped, as sweat from his body dripped onto mine, his fast and furious fucking taking me over the edge. My legs came into the air and wrapped around him as he pounded into me, making me cum so hard, so strongly, feeling his balls slapping against me as his pace increased further. He was making my ass so raw as he fucked me, he made me pant, beg for more… beg for his cum.

'I'm gonna cum!' he breathed, whispering into my ear. 'Where do you want it? chest? Face?'

'Inside of me!' I begged. 'Dump your cum deep in my ass! I want it Greg, I want your cum! Fucking cum inside of me now!'

His back arched, his face contorted as he came, his legs shook just as his balls tightened, his cock bounding inside of my tight hole - his hot cum exploding deep inside of my ass until we lay breathless, his cock still twitching in me, still delivering those last few drops of his sweet cum.

We laid together and cuddled for a while, until he suddenly stood up, his cock at half mast. 'Now, we swim' he announced. 'We swim until we're tired, and then we fuck again. Deal?'

'Deal' I answered, happily.

# CHAPTER 8
# DIRTY BOY

LET ME SET THE SCENE... tell you exactly what's going on right now. Let me tell you why I'm the luckiest twink boy in the whole fucking country right now.

I'm on my knees. I'm naked. I have my boyfriend in front of me, holding my head in place as I deep-throat on his cock, streams of my saliva dripping off his shaft as he feeds that hard dick deep into my mouth. I'm gagging on him, tugging gently on his swinging balls as he throat fucks me, rocking back and forth as I bring him close to orgasm. My mind full of swirling emotions as I wonder if he'll cum in my mouth, or if he'll pull out and shoot onto my face.

Behind me, the man next door is kneeling, pressing his thick cock against the entrance of my gaping lubed up asshole. As I suck on my boyfriend he's stroking his shaft, getting himself hard before plunging his thick rod deep into me. It makes me groan with pleasure as his palms slap down onto my ass cheeks, gripping my flesh - running his hands from my ass to my hardening cock and sending me over the edge as I feel my orgasm start to roll throughout my body.

And to my immediate left, sitting on the couch - his husband. Yes, I live next door to a gay couple and it's fucking awesome. You know, I used to live in a more conservative state... but since moving north it's been amazing. There's married gay couples. There's plenty of guys for a boy like me to fuck.

Anyway... back to the story. He is also naked, his legs spread - offering his hard cock to my fingers. He's stroking himself, watching as his husband plows into the young twink babysitter - encouraging him - telling him how hot this all is, how he should cum inside of my tight asshole. He wants to watch, he wants to watch me being throat fucked by my boyfriend while his husband slams into me - he wants to taste the cum of both men directly from my body, my mouth, and my ass.

Let's just say that this isn't exactly a normal Tuesday for me.

Everything started off as normal. I've been babysitting for the Thomas family for a couple of years now, even though I'm 20 years old and have a 'proper' job, I like babysitting.

What's not to like? They live next door, so it's not like I have any commuting to do. The kids are old enough so if they're awake when I get there I just tell them when it's bedtime and the go upstairs and go straight to sleep - and then I'm free to do whatever I want. I can watch TV, I can log onto their wifi and play online on my phone, I can make myself something to eat or something to drink, and I can let my boyfriend in and suck his cock - all while being paid.

Okay, okay... I don't know if I'm exactly allowed to have my boyfriend over and I've always been pretty sure that they might have a few choice words to say. I always saw them as being pretty prim and proper - old school gay is how my boyfriend described them - and imagine that if they ever walked in and saw me with a cock in my mouth, then this easy gig would fly out of the window.

That's... not exactly what happened. I guess looking back on it, the clues were there - I just hadn't picked up on them.

Nothing was normal. They don't usually ask me to babysit on a Tuesday. They usually go out for dinner or to see a movie on a Friday or Saturday night. Plus, whenever I usually go over there, they're dressed nicely, but casual. They are the kind of couple who don't go out to an expensive restaurant but instead go to a chain place and sit at the bar, eating appetisers.

Tonight, on a Tuesday, they looked a lot different. John had on a black suit. No tie, but a crisp white shirt. The top two buttons were undone, revealing a tanned hairy chest that I had never seen before. This was a guy that I was used to seeing in a t-shirt and jeans and I hadn't ever really paid attention to him before - but this outfit and the confidence that it gave to him allowed me to see him in a different light.

Honestly, I was kind of attracted to him. He was hot.

His baggy clothes that he usually wears covers him up so much. But this look? The clothes fit so well, and let me see that he actually has a really good figure. He stood taller, he wasn't hunched like he usually is. I saw him and suddenly felt a bunch of hormones rushing around my body - thinking that if he said something like, oh - I don't know - 'Hey Leo, do you want to suck my fat cock?' then I would have dropped to my knees and unzipped him and fed that cock into my mouth.

But he wasn't the only one who looked a lot different. John let me in and smiled at me, and as we stood in the hallway I heard his husband, Anthony, coming down the stairs.

I don't usually hear him walking. He's often dressed kind of frumpy, and wears pretty similar clothes to his husband. I've never seen him as someone who takes care of himself or makes any real attempt to look good. Tonight though?

Well, like I said, my first clue was what I heard. As I stood in the hallway with John I heard the unmistakable sound of leather dress shoes walking down the wooden staircase. As I turned to see Anthony, I was struck by how good he looked.

He was wearing a long thick black coat, which covered whatever he was wearing underneath but he carried himself with such confidence that he practically glided across the floor towards us. I could see that he was also wearing a nice pair of suit pants, and could see the shiny black shoes that I could hear above us when he made his entrance. As he reached me I took a deep breath, letting the scent of his cologne fill my nostrils.

'Damn guys' I said in wonder with my mouth open. 'You both look amazing!'

'Thanks!' Anthony said. 'We hope that the other people think the same'.

I fucking swear that he gave me a wink when he said that.

I really wasn't planning on having my boyfriend over tonight. Like I've said, I have asked him to come over when I'm there but it honestly always makes me feel a little bit guilty and I really don't want to get caught by John and Anthony. This is a good little job! They pay me well...

But, after seeing how John and Anthony looked - after smelling their cologne, feeling their confidence and watching them walking arm in arm to their car, I was overcome with hormones and emotions.

Basically, I needed cock and my boyfriend was happy to supply his.

I waited for - oh - about five minutes before plucking my phone out of my pocket and texting Steven.

'Hey' I typed. 'I'm babysitting tonight'.

'Do you need anything?' he responded.

'Yes' - I typed back. 'Your cock. Hard. In my mouth. Is that okay?'

I swear that I heard car tires screeching as soon as I pressed send.

He knew the rules, he parked around the corner and came

around the back of the house. I opened the back door and let him in, putting my finger to my lips to make sure that he knew to keep quiet.

He would do anything I told him to do - he knew what he was getting out of the deal here. He had a massive smile on his face and a bulge in his pants as he followed me into the living room.

'Did you bring me what I asked for?' I said, starting to unbutton my shirt - feeling my cock getting excited. A warm glow came over me as I took off my shirt and let it fall to the floor beside me.

'It's right here' he said, gripping the meat of his cock through his pants - showing me that he was already getting hard.

I'm usually a little more careful, I usually make sure that I can dress myself quickly if the need arises but tonight I just didn't give a fuck and as soon as I was topless, I also pulled down my pants. My underpants came down with them - leaving me standing there totally naked in front of him, my cock already getting hard, my ass feeling like it was already excited and starting to gape in anticipation.

'Damn Leo' he said - a wide grin on his face. He quickly stripped, taking his t-shirt off with one sexy movement and then pulling down his pants. I walked over to him - wrapping my arms around my boyfriend - pulling him towards me and kissing him - my tongue flicking his, my teeth biting his bottom lip. His hands came to my bare ass - squeezing my cheeks - his fingers reaching to spread my ass and stroke my puckering asshole from behind. I knew that I was getting hungry for cock already and knew that his fingers would be covered the heat of my ass and my scent, so I wrapped my fingers around the band of his underwear and tugged them down - releasing his cock.

He gasped as I took his length in my hand - stroking the skin of his cock - feeling it harden in my palm. My hands were a little cold as I teased him, making his cock grow as I prepared it for my mouth. His fingers were now reaching inside of my hot dark asshole, coating themselves so much with my musk that I ran one hand down my body, gripping my cock, squeezing my sensitive balls as I reached his wrist. I stepped back, releasing my grip on his cock and took his hand to bring it to my mouth - taking one musk covered finger and licking it, sucking on it, tasting myself on him as I brought that finger to the back of my throat.

I've always enjoyed deep throating. I first experimented with a dildo and while it initially felt a little uncomfortable and I did gag a bit, I found (to my surprise) that I enjoyed it. A lot. I could basically cum just by sucking on a dildo and feeding it down my throat - I hardly had to touch my dick at all.

Dildo's are fine and all... but tonight I was able to deep throat the real thing and I didn't want to waste any time. I dropped to my knees and stroked that meaty cock above my head - delving my tongue into his balls - taking one into my warm mouth and sucking on it while gripping his cock - stroking him - before opening up my mouth to take him whole.

I could feel his hands on my head - holding me in place as he liked to do - his hips slowly gyrating, feeding his cock deeper into my mouth as my lips wrapped around him. He throat fucked me so deep that his swinging balls kissed my chin, covering themselves in the streams of saliva that were escaping out of the corner of my mouth. The room was so filled with the sounds of my gagging on his cock and by his groans as he came so close to cumming that we couldn't hear anything else - we certainly didn't hear the front door opening, we didn't hear footsteps, we didn't know that we weren't alone until we heard a man clearing his throat.

'Ahem'.

That was a sound which stopped me in my tracks. A cold

shiver travelled throughout my naked body as the realization that I'd be caught came over me. I let Steve's cock slowly slip out of my mouth and turned my head to see my next door neighbors - Anthony and his husband John standing in the doorway.

Smiling.

I told you that this was no ordinary Tuesday.

There really wasn't anything that I could do to cover myself up or deny what was happening. When they walked in I had a cock in my mouth. I was entirely naked. My cock and my balls were swinging just inches from their new living room carpet.

'So… uh… I guess I'm fired, right?' I said, still on all fours with a rapidly shrinking cock just in front of my face. I had a sinking feeling in the pit of my stomach, knowing that my life had somehow changed in that moment.

I looked over at John and Anthony, my face turning a bright shade of red. They stood there - both still smiling. They turned to each other, smiled and kind of shrugged in a 'why not' kind of way and turned back to us.

'So, there's something we should tell you' John said as they both walked towards us. Anthony looked so excited as he took a seat on the sofa, still wearing his coat, his legs just inches away from my face as his husband came behind me - standing there with a prime look at my ass and my swinging balls. 'We didn't go on one of our usual dates…'

He knelt behind me, one nervous palm coming to rest on the base of my back, just a finger length away from my ass. I could tell that he didn't know if I was okay with him touching me so I gave him some encouragement - letting a small sigh leave my lips and bringing one hand to take his and slide it towards my ass cheek.

'We were going to meet a couple' Anthony said, finally opening up his black coat to show me - and Steve - what she was wearing underneath. Based on how John was dressed, I had assumed that he would be wearing the same kind suit or something… so it came as quite a shock when I saw that underneath that coat he was wearing pants, but they were cut to reveal his cock. He was totally letting it all hang out and was already getting hard as he watched me kneeling naked on his living room floor. Like I said I've never really felt all that attracted to him but seeing him like that? I kind of wanted to know how his cock tasted. 'We were going to… fuck this couple. But just as we were getting to the hotel they bailed on us. We figured we would just come back here and have sex with each other but…'

Oh god, was this really going the way that I thought it was going? My asshole certainly seemed to want it to go that way… and my hand that was holding onto Anthony's wrist and was now motioning his fingers to stroke my puckering, almost gaping asshole seemed to want the same thing too…

'Fuck me' I said, looking over my shoulder at John, looking at his husband while I leaned back to suck on the cock of my boyfriend. 'Fuck me hard, fuck me fast - just fuck me while I suck on this cock!'

Anthony seemed so excited, so happy - he sat back on the sofa and opened his legs, showing me his delicately shaved raw asshole as he brought his fingers to his thick hard cock - stroking himself and watching as his husband unzipped his pants to bring his cock towards me. I felt his fingers rushing inside of my asshole, rolling and turning and curling and prodding - pulling apart my cheeks in preparation for his thick cock. I let my mouth hang open and filled my face with Steve's cock once more - letting him fill me the fuck up as I gagged again on my boyfriend.

'Yes!' Anthony screamed as he watched his husband enter into me. His cock stretched me wide and made me groan as my tight asshole walls gripped onto his fat shaft. 'Yes my man! fuck him! I wanna watch you fuck this twink boy!'

John began to bring his hands up and opened his palms,

bringing them down swiftly to slap my ass cheeks - making me groan, gush, and bringing me even closer to a massive orgasm. The cock in my mouth grew suddenly harder as my boyfriend neared his goal - as I gagged deep on his dick he suddenly withdrew and stroked himself to completion, shooting his hot cum onto my face, hitting my eyes, my nose and my lips.

Anthony squealed with delight as he watched me being covered with cum - he leaned towards me - taking my head in his hands and coming at me with an open mouth, his tongue coming to lap cum away from my eyes and my forehead before kissing me tenderly, his tongue licking my lips and then going deep into my mouth - making out with me and taking the cum of my boyfriend for himself while his husband fucked me deep and hard and fast. I let my hand come to his groin - sliding two fingers into his open asshole and fingering him in time with his husband behind me - he shifted himself to the edge of the sofa while I banged his asshole then he laid back, spread his legs open wide and grabbed my head to bring me into his most private area. I felt a massive orgasm take over me as I dove on him - my mouth filled with the scent of his ass as my tongue dipped deep inside of him - rimming him without hesitation as he held my head in place just as my boyfriend had done on his cock as I licked him out, tasting his scent as he stroked himself and came on my face. Tony looked on in pleasure as he picked up his speed and slammed his fat dick into me, stretching me - groaning as his balls slapped on my ass - as his cock exploded inside of me - filling me with his hot cum. Leaning over the back of my body his mouth met mine at his husbands bobbing cock, us both licking the cum from his shaft.

Not the usual Tuesday... like I said. There's a big part of me that hopes that it will be a regular fixture though - and when we were all dressed and were sharing a bottle of wine we talked about how much fun we had had together.

www.ingramcontent.com/pod-product-compliance
Lightning Source LLC
Chambersburg PA
CBHW031452130726
47989CB00003B/1348